The Angel Manuscripts

die Gefallenen

THE BOOK OF ZURIEL,

PART I

Seth Underwood

The Angel Manuscripts
die Gefallenen – The Book of Zuriel, Part I
Genre of Book- Biblical Mythopoeia

Copyright © 2016-2017 by AEM Services. All rights reserved. No part of this book may be used or reproduced in any manner whatsoever without written permission except in the case of brief quotation embodied in critical articles and reviews. For information contact contact@angelmanuscripts.com.

Publishers Note- The story, all names, characters, and incidents portrayed in this book are fictitious. Names, characters, places, and incidents are a product of the author's imagination. Locales and public names are sometimes used for atmospheric purposes. No identification with actual persons (living or deceased), places, buildings, and products is intended or should be inferred. Any names associated with http://www.fantasynamegenerators.com/ in no way represent ownership over said names as a trade mark or otherwise.

Cover Art, Graphics and Photos Provided by extended license from Adobe Stock, FILE #84413169, © zwiebackesser/stock.adobe.com; FILE #: 114073130, © paffy/stock.adobe.com; David Maydoney; Anna Martin; NASA, ESA, the Hubble Heritage Team (STScI/AURA); and Canva.com. Any and all copyrights associated remain with their respective owners.

Icon Image of Aya ("Image") Copyright owned by Colette M. Kalvesmaki.

ISBN 9781973309697

ISBN 13: 978-0692070642 (AEM Services)

78 111 116 104 105 110 103 32 105 115 32 97 115 32 105 116 32 115 101 101 109 115 32 111 114 32 97 112 112 101 97 114 115 46 13 10 70 97 107 101 110 101 115 115 32 105 115 32 101 97 115 121 46 13 10 84 114 117 116 104 32 105 115 32 104 97 114 100 46

LIKE US ON FACEBOOK

Check out the latest information on the die Gefallenen – The Book of Zuriel on Seth Underwood's Facebook Page – https://www.facebook.com/seth.underwood.author/

Links and information can be found there about the codes, the Nazi Archeologist Otto von Hemrick and much more. Check it out. www.angelmanuscripts.com

Part II of the series covering the period time just before Jesus through the New Testament Period will be next. Precursor translations will appear on the website and Facebook Page.

Don't Forget to Leave a Review
And
Recommend us to your Friends and Family
And
Leave a Post on Reddit's
WEEKLY "WHAT ARE YOU READING?" THREAD!

is = 105,115

A Personal Prayer to St. Michael the Archangel

*St. Michael the Archangel, be our guide on our
spiritual journey. Send forth your heavenly Army to
defend us against the Legions of the Satan and all his
Temptations. And Thrust back into the Depths of Hell
for all Eternity all Spirits that would cause harm to us.
Amen.*

Anonymous

Table of Contents

During the summer of 1923, Otto von Hemrick, a Nazi archeologist of the Ahnenerbe, was excavating in the ruins of a 4th Century Christian Monastery somewhere outside of modern Djouaniye east of the town of Armanaz in Syria, when he discovered die Gefallenen (the Book of Zuriel).

He took these discoveries back to Germany where he worked on the translation of the cryptic language they contained, which he called "Muttersprache" or mother language. With the aid of a couple Nazi code breakers, and an "enigma machine," they were able to develop a translation matrix. von Hemrick noted that some of the words did not translate exactly into German, but instead into transliterated Hebrew, which perplexed and disturbed him a bit. Undeterred, he continued to translate the text section by section to determine what hidden knowledge it contained. It was from these texts that he was able to develop a scientific experiment which unfortunately would end his own life.

As WWII ended and Germany fell, die Gefallenen along with von Hemrick's notes and other materials were gathered up by an American GI and were shipped to the United States. During the 1960s, all the materials that the American GI had gathered were donated to the Catholic University of America where they sat in several boxes labeled "Angel Manuscripts" until I came across them during my doctoral research.

It is clear that these texts are predicting some future events or recently occurred events through various cryptic codes of numbers and word substitutions (which I have yet to really figure out). Through my work with the Catholic Committee on Biblical Transliteration, I have learned from Deacon Mahdi that these texts were part of a group of a spiritual writing originally in the possession of Simon the Lesser, who was a follower of Simon of Peraea (a precursor Messiah figure who died in 4 BCE). Simon the Lesser joined John the Baptist's movement until his death, and then joined the Jesus' followers. According to Deacon Mahdi, legends report that St. Peter brought the texts along with other texts to Antioch and later that Ignatius the Illuminator was supposed to have preached from them. The texts were then buried during the Syrian Genocide of 1915. What is truly amazing is that despite being clearly some form of Gnostic or Docetae texts, the fact that they were part of an early Christian tradition clearly allowed them to survive during the reign of Roman Emperor Theodosius the First when much of Pagan and Gnostic literature was lost. Third and lastly, die Gefallenen is not the only text in the boxes at CUA. There are at least two more as far as I can tell, although Deacon Mahdi says there should have been more; All of them being written in that cryptic language von Hemrick called the mother language.

The origins of Gnosticism or gnosis is still being debated. Most
contemporary scholars agree it started to develop sometime around
the 1st and 2nd century. This is when we have the first true historical
mention of the issue with the writings of St. Irenaeus (c. 185 AD)
countering various Gnostic heresies brought up during his time.
There were many different schools of gnosis at this time with various
ideas concerning creation, issues of spiritual vs. material existence,
and other similar thoughts and all apparently using a wide variety of
texts as confirmed by St. Irenaeus. One could make an argument that
in some ways early Christianity had a competitor where the religions
of the old gods of Rome were being merged into the newly
developing Christianity making a new religion combined. A new
metaphysical religion, not wanting to be outdone by the growing
religion of Christianity, including merging elements of Christianity
into it with the most famous version being Manichaeism.

One could almost make an argument that the seeds of Gnosticism
were already present within the spirituality of Judaism in that the
spiritual ideas of the one true God, and the Messiah by the time of the
1st Century CE. We see this well represented in communities such as
those who developed the Dead Sea Scrolls where various alternative
texts are available. This is not to mention the well-known Book of
Enoch, which is referenced in the Jude 1:14 There are also many
other missing texts in the Bible, which never made it into the canon
of the Bible but are referenced. These divisions of schools of thought
cause issues within a religion to the exact nature of that religion and
what is its official beliefs and origin of divine inspiration.

With Docetae, derived from the word dokesis (which means to
seem), this is a specific earlier version of Christian-style gnosis
dealing with Christ's incarnate nature, or His birth, or His death and
life, or all three. In Docetae it is a full denial of these aspects of
Christ. This heresy was taken on by the Bishop of Antioch around
190-203 CE in the letter of Serapion, but evidence indicates that this
issue was dealt with even earlier in the Church's history, including in
the Bible itself, where we see the writings of St. Paul dealing with the

fullness of the Godhead and Christ in Colossians 1:19, 2:9, as well as St. John dealing with this specific heresy in 1 John 1:1-3, 4:1-3; 2 John 7.

In 325 Constantine I and the Council of Nicea make Christianity the official religion of Rome, and by 381 Theodosius I begin the campaign of wiping out all vestiges of the old pagan religions of Rome as well as anything that was heterodoxy to Christianity which included any Gnostic texts or texts that were now not accepted as official cannon by the official Christian Church. This campaign continues up to 392 just a few years from Theodosius I's death in 395 CE. The decrees he orders called for book burnings, temple destructions and a host of other "cleansings" including the death of heretics. Some have speculated that this period of time is spoken of in the Book of Revelations as the reign of 1000 years of Jesus and his followers (Rev. 20:4). With the level of destruction that occurred during this time period, it is amazing that any material has survived to the modern era.

This brings up a most interesting problem; that what has survived into the modern era are texts that were found in places like Egypt starting in the late 1890s going through the mid-20th Century. The largest find being that of Oxyrhynchus Papyri found back around 1898 by Bernard Pyne Grenfell and Arthur Surridge Hunt in what was a garbage mound in Oxyrhynchus Egypt. This finding alone is still being decoded and reviewed to this day for it contains thousands of pages of materials ranging from basic tax and property records to Greek plays to the Books of Spells to Gnostic Texts. This finding alone has primarily contributed almost all that we know of the Gnostic and early world in addition to later the finds of the Nagi Hammadi library in 1945. Without these texts we can only speculate on what was believed and understood from such writings as St. Irenaeus. So the question becomes though, why were these finds so late in time? In theory, with the level of destruction that happened back during the Theodosius I campaign, there really shouldn't be almost anything left by the late 1890s, begging the question are some of these text forgeries? It would be far easier back in the late 1890s and early 1900s to make a forgery than it is today, and having a trash mound of ancient papyri does help. Not that I am saying this is what was done, but even as the famous "Crystal Skulls" in the London and

Parish museums have been found to be fake and they came from the same late 1890s time period when museums paid handsomely for such finds. Archeology back in this time period and even during the time period of Otto von Hemrick was not as scientific and meticulous as it is today, and fakes were common place. Could these texts by Otto von Hemrick be faked as well? Made up just to save his own life or increase his own prestige during a time of war? It is very possible, but for Otto von Hemrick it didn't turn out that way.

My point with all this is as follows, when it comes to texts that are Gnostic, Docatae, or any text that is **NOT** officially recognized as divinely inspired or cannon of a religion- you can read them but don't believe them as **Truth**. And this would apply to die Gefallenen - the Book of Zuriel as well.

die Gefallenen or the Book of Zuriel is basically broken into two parts- The Old Testament period and the New Testament period, and this specific book deals with the Old Testament period. The Book of Zuriel appears to be missing passages referring to certain Old Testament periods, for example, Exodus through the creation of the Davidic Kingdoms and the splitting up of the Jewish Kingdoms. Also missing are those classic Genesis stories that deal with angels like Sodom and Gomorra. This may have been done intentionally to avoid the destruction of the text by Thaddeus I, or it is possible that these parts were left out because they served no purpose to the spiritual message being conveyed. What is known is that there are references to some events leading up to Exodus occurring during the Jewish exile in Egypt as some sort of a joint campaign between the "Good Angels" and the "Fallen Angels." Unfortunately, we may never know more since this period is missing from the translations.

The individual chapters can be grouped into broad sections corresponding to various Old Testament periods/themes or major time periods for the Jewish peoples as follows-

Early Genesis Period

Chapter 1 Die Anfänge - The Beginnings, with the creation of Zuriel and the angels.

Chapter 2 Die Entstehung der Erde - The Formation of the Earth, an expansion on the first few lines Genesis 1.

Chapter 3 Stolz von Winkeln - Pride of Angels, seems to explain elements of the spiritual universe like the Abyss.

Chapter 4 Die Sünde des Menschen - Sin of Man, an expansion on the fall of man in Genesis.

Chapter 5 Von Riesen und Hochwasser - From Floods and Giants, a different take on the great flood in Genesis.

Middle Genesis Period

Chapter 6 Ursprung der Unanständigkeit - Origin of Indecency, a new development on the story dealing with Noah.

Chapter 7 Jakob und der Gefallenen - Jacob and the Fallen, a re-interpretation of Jacob's wrestling with an angel.

Chapter 8 Gebogenen Stange Völker - The Bent Rod People, an extension of Onan and foretelling of the coming of the Nazis party.

Late Genesis Period

Chapter 10 Gesicht Gottes - Face of God, this begins a four-part prophetic section expanding off the first part of the Book of Job.

Reisen Sie zurück in den Himmel- Travel Back to Heaven, a retelling of the Satan's return to Heaven in the first part of the Book of Job.

Dichtungen, Trompeten und Schalen - Seals, Trumpets and Bowls, an enlargement on the mysteries of the book of Revelation.

Das Wahrsagen des Christus und der Krieg - The Foretelling of the Christ and the War, the Satan details the Gnostic view of Christ.

Ende der Menschheit- The End of Humanity, the Satan explains how he will destroy humanity.

Exodus Period

The next chapter is technically out of order in the known timeline of the Bible. This could be because of how the text was edited by previous scribes to show some sort of emphasis of a school of thought.

Chapter 9 Ehe von Mann - Marriage of Man, deals with marriage and divorce. It could belong to the Early Genesis Period as a continuation of Chapters 4-5 of the text. Or this section could also be referring to a possible later period dealing with Moses' allowance of divorce. I suspect it is more in reference to the allowance of divorce by Moses, and may represent the only text reference to the Exodus Period.

Fall of the Jewish Kingdoms and Exile to Babylon Period

Chapter 11 Wächter Vogel - Guardian Bird, how the Davidic Kingdoms fell and the beginning of a war in Heaven.

Chapter 12 Amerikas Zerstörung - Destruction of America, a prophetic vision of how the priests of the followers of God in America will be eternally sad. Appears to relate to 2 Kings 9:27 and Isaiah 24, plus some personal reflective material from the writer Zuriel.

Chapter 14 die Hexe - The Witch, or the introduction of demoness Lilith and how she will be used by the Satan, especially during a suspected future period of time. Appears to be related to the Book of Daniel but also contains again some personal thoughts from Zuriel.

Chapter 15 Weisheit - Wisdom, is a conversation between the Satan and Zuriel over the nature of the material-spiritual world. This part was added in at a later date or contributed by another author.

Chapter 16 Drachen und Löwen - Dragon and Lions, deals with Prophet Daniel, the Archangel Raphael, and parts from the book of Tobit. It clearly shows how the Satan "cares" for his own minions.

Chapter 17 die Zwei - The Two, deals with dualism, Zurvanist Zoroastrianism (extinct heretical branch of Zoroastrianism), and Baruch.

Chapter 18 Engel des Dieners - The Angels of the Servant, deals with the prophetic Book of Obadiah, where Zuriel has a conversation with four Cherubim. (Codes Present)

Chapter 19 die klagende Sohn - The Lamenting Son, deals with a combination of the Second Testament Parable of the Prodigal Son and also Chapter 3 of Lamentations in the Old Testament. We see Zuriel ponders the mystery of human lamenting.

Chapter 1

Die Anfänge

(The Beginnings)

The first group of writings translated is what is known as "the beginnings" mainly because it is describing some initial events of the author, Zuriel.

1 Darkness.

2 All is darkness. But I am not alone. There are others here as well. There is also a rushing wind below me. From above I heard my name called. 'Zuriel come up here.' I fumbled up some stairs into what was more darkness, but again I was not alone. I could sense others standing around me just as confused as I was.

3 A voice from above spoke, 'Hosek, move the Achim to the main deck and await further instructions.' 'Yes, Adonai' came from the voice that called me.

4 I felt the others pressing on me as we moved forward and up some sort of ramp to a level surface.

5 Again everything was still darkness, and I could still hear that wind below us all. That rushing wind that never seems to go away, blowing over something fluid.

6 "Here eat this. It will taste bitter, but will allow you to see and end the confusion." It was very bitter to the taste, but my mind cleared. I

could finally see around me the lines of Achim standing and waiting.

7 In front of us was a towering structure, from which there were four creatures at the top. There were others there as well, but I could not make out their form. I saw Hosek distributing more of that bitter paper.

8 All was in preparation. From the tower came down some of the Akim; they were like us, Achim, but looked different. They were more slender and taller. They were known as the architects and designers of Adonai. Part of Adonai's inner circle a top of the tower. I saw them with Hosek, and another of the Achim leaders, Elisheva, on the deck of the Oniya.

9 Yago, my companion on the Oniya, told me he overheard Hosek speaking with the Akim. Hosek didn't seem too pleased with what they were saying.

10 According to Yago, a new craft is to be built, the Kli. It will be smaller than the Oniya and some of the Akim are to go with it in preparation for the plans of the Akim for what lies below the winds.

11 A day of choice.

12 The Akim gathered all the Achim upon the main deck of the Oniya. Standing before them was Hosek and Elisheva. Nearby one could see the Kli we had constructed with the help of the Akim.

13 From above Adonai spoke, "Choose Achim. Do you go with Hosek? Or with Elisheva?" About two thirds went with Elisheva to stay on the Oniya. I could not decide so easily.

14 Hosek stood before me and forcefully commanded "What of you Zuriel?! Choose as Adonai has said!" I quickly muttered, "I choose to go with my friend Yago. I choose to be with Hosek."

15 Thus my choice was made to go with Hosek aboard the Kli.

16 In my spirit's heart though I felt some pity for the Achim for going with Elisheva, as I watched those Achim who went with Elisheva given new armor which glowed with a brilliance that hurt the eyes; From that day forward those with Elisheva were known as Uri for the glow of their armor.

Chapter 2

Die Entstehung der Erde

(the Origin of the Earth)

*According to von Hemrick's notes the next part he called the Origin of
the Earth. von Hemrick's notes are more fragmented here, but I have
tried to put things in an order that makes sense.*

1 We prepared the Kli for its voyage. Yago said
some special equipment was being brought on
board from the Tower. He thought they were
weapons.

2 I was stationed on the command deck of the
Kli. I was responsible for navigation, although I
had no idea where we were going exactly.

3 The voyage began. I took my station, and
with me were Hosek and some of the Akim as
well as about four other Achim to operate the
controls. Yago was assigned to the engines.

4 Hosek and the Akim put the Kli through its
testing trails. It seemed like we were going
nowhere for a very long time.

5 Now I think the real mission will begin soon.
I had heard Hosek and the Akim arguing
privately in room adjacent to the command
area.

6 I am troubled. I have learned we are to
venture past the ever blowing winds into the
chaos that is Toho Erets. All I know is there is

nothing but water there and below its depths the Tehom of imaginable chaos.

7 I honestly think we will be ripped to shreds by the winds before we even get to Toho Erets. Even if we make it past the winds, there is no way to guide the Kli through the watery chaos of Toho Erets.

8 Yago says that nothing works there and all that you know is turned upside down. No wonder Hosek didn't want to go, but why are the Akim taking us there? There is nothing there for us.

9 I know I shouldn't doubt Adonai or his Akim, but this makes no sense and seems fool hardy. I honestly think we are being sentenced to death.

10 Hosek gave the order to make our way through the winds to Toho Erets. All on the command deck sat there with a look of 'are you sure?' But I set the course and we hit the winds hard. The whole of the Kli shook violently as the winds tore at its sides.

11 The gleaming lights of the armor of the Uri aboard the Oniya faded quickly from sight, replaced by a dark violent wind. We were all tossed from side to side as the winds battered the Kli.

12 Eventually we made it through and hit the surface of Toho Erets. The Kli suffered damage when it hit the surface.

13 Today we made many repairs. The Akim were busy preparing the equipment brought on board. Yago said it looked like a large pod of some kind. He still thinks it's a weapon.

14 The readings I was getting as we sat on the surface of the Toho Erets were just strange. My training had not prepared me for such things. There were large fluctuations. Nothing was stable like above the Winds. I couldn't even get our bearing. Although for a moment or two I saw something in the Tehom region. Something stable, but it flickered out.

Chapter 3

Stolz von Winkeln

(Pride of Angels)

This section appears related to the creation section, but is disjointed. I have no idea why von Hemrick's notes call it the "Pride of Angels." Pride is a complex word in the English language. It can mean a certain joyful feeling in your own accomplishments or that of others. But it can also mean a false feeling of joy due to one's hubris in self or something.

1 I asked Yago once if he saw the nothingness. He said he did, as did the others on the Kli. He said it made him and many others just angry that the future was filled with such nothingness. For myself, I was uncertain what to feel.

2 I wondered what the Uri saw. Could they not see the nothingness as well? To know that the nothingness is all that will be in the end, how could they just blindly follow a path which will end thusly?

3 We are all alone and cut off in the end. Why should we trust in a path of chaos and randomness? Sometimes I just don't understand Adonai's orders for us. They make no sense.

4 I agree with Hosek. We must all make our own path. Sure we should do Adonai's will or follow the Akim, but not when it does not make sense. You can obviously see the end of such a path, and it leads nowhere.

5 While the Akim were making preparations, Hosek ordered me to come with him deeper into Toho Erets to the Tehom.

6 We were buffeted by the chaos of the Toho Erets, but finally made it to the Tehom. It was odd in the Tehom. A certain calm was present, but still the readings were odd. I also noticed something moving outside the window.

7 I asked Hosek about them, and he said they were the creatures of the Tehom – the Tsale. They were nothing to worry about or be concerned with. I was unaware that they even existed, and they were like us but not at the same time. Like a ghost image or reflection.

8 Hosek ordered me to stay while he went outside into the Tehom alone. He said he needed to take some readings. I saw him in the Tehom through the window. Those Tsale were swarming around him but he waved them away.

9 Then I noticed on my readings something really stable in front of us. About where Hosek was he appeared to be talking to something or someone, but his communications link was turned off. Eventually he came back, and appeared to be putting something in his pocket. I asked Hosek about the readings, and he said not to worry about it and to go back to the Kli.

Chapter 4

Die Sünde des Menschen

(Sin of Man)

This section is called the Sin of Man. It appears to be related to the creation of the earth part, in that it opens with what appears to be the mechanism for the creation of the universe mentioned in the earlier part as the pod shaped device. Surreal is showing a more explanative version of the events mentioned in Genesis dealing with the curses laid upon the Satan, the woman, and the man. It is a fascinating new tradition into these events, assuming the translation matrix is accurate.

1 We were told by the Akim that the Dabar will be activated soon upon the commands from the Tower, and that we should expect some extreme changes to occur.

2 Changes? What do they mean by changes? What was the Tower up to? What more could they do to this place than what is already here? It is nothing but a sea of change.

3 My mind was restless. I could not sleep knowing what was to come, so I took a little walk. There I saw Hosek dimly with the Dabar. He took something from his pocket and put it into the Dabar. I quickly left before he could see me watching.

4 Word came from the Tower, and the Dabar was activated. The whole of the Kli shook like it was going to come apart at the seams. It was like the ever blowing wind above was being sucked into the ship.

5 The change started off small but then grew larger and larger. Then in an instance the readings all changed in the Toho Erets. Outside there was no more swirling chaos, there was no more ever blowing wind above, but things seem to come more into order.

6 The Akim said the first phase had been completed, and now we were looking upon the Tsaatsuim Erets that was planned. My readings still showed the Tehom as unchanged.

7 The following day, the Akim came up to Hosek. They were obviously agitated about something. They were talking about something being introduced into the Dabar.

8 A change from the original designs from the Tower. After some heated exchanges between them and Hosek, some of the Akim left the Kli to return to the Onyia to report their findings."

9 It was not for a day until new instructions were sent from the Tower. Those on the Kli were to stay in the Tsaatsuim Erets until further notice.

10 Hosek that day was not in a pleasant mood, and we tried our best to stay out of his way.

11 Yago told me a rumor has it that Hosek was seriously reprimanded by Adonai and that is why we are all stuck here not to return to the Onyia. I held my tongue about what I saw Hosek do to the Dabar.

12 I overheard the remaining Akim and Hosek talking about some further changes that will come to the Dabar so the second phase could be completed.

13 Something to do with the creation of the Akamu who are to care for the Tsaatsuim Erets. The problem deals with bachar being given to the Akamu.

14 I thought only we Achim had the bachar. The introduction of chalal and zehman was needed to correct the problem.

15 I really didn't understand what they meant by chalal and zehman. It sounded like some sort of substance.

Chapter 5

Von Riesen und Hochwasser

(Of Giants and Floods)

von Hemrick's notes calls this section "Of Giants and Floods" while the text is pretty cut up, I have tried to arrange it in something more familiar. This part seems to elaborate on the part of Genesis dealing with the formation of heroes (i.e. Giants) as well as adding some interesting takes on the flood itself. This docetae tradition is trying to show the nature of our spiritual selves and how God was cleansing the Earth of not just human evil but evil in general.

Of course, my friend Alyssa, once told me that she thought the flood in Genesis was recalling not just some sort of local flood, but possibly the genetic bottleneck that happened to the human species some 50,000 years ago when only a few humans survived a great cataclysm. This might be, but such ideas are not the accepted origins of the flood in the Bible.

As an aside, von Hemrick's notes seem to concentrate on issues of the Giants as some form of earlier super-race. He postulates in his notes that there may be some way to recreate the infusion mentioned in the text, and thus remake this original super-race.

1 According to Yago, after watching the development of the Akamu for some time, those Akim who had remained on the Kli seemed to be extremely fascinated with the Akamu ishshah and the nebarbeyheem they could see within them.

2 I had no idea what the Akim saw in these Akamu. To me they were just some odd creatures of the Tsaatsium Erets.

3 The Akim had contacted the Tower and asked to perform some modifications to the Dabar to allow a portion of their spirit to be incorporated into some of the Akamu ishshah.

4 Hosek was upset today with the Akim. They got approval for their modifications, but under one qualification that a more zehman was added to limit the modifications.

5 Hosek called the Tower afterwards asking permission to collect the nebarbeyheem from the Akamu due to the presence of zehman.

6 I still don't understand what the issue is with the zehman or why Hosek wants us now to collect it the nebarbeyheems from the Akamu. Who am I to question Hosek? His vision is better than mine from what I understand. Some say he was the first among the Achim.

7 After the modification was executed, the remaining Akim left the Kli to be with the Akamu ibriy as they were now known. That was the last we saw of the Akim.

8 Yago was complaining that Hosek was having them make extensive modifications to the Dabar left behind by the Akim.

9 Hosek was really riding them to get the modifications completed as quickly as possible. Afterwards, under Hosek's orders, they jettisoned the Dabar into the Tehom.

10 Hosek ordered us to land the Kli onto the surface of the Tsaatsium Erets.

11 Afterwards he ordered us to disembark and then all the Achim were given the means to collect the neharbeyheem from the Akamu.

12 We were carefully instructed by Hosek that we should return to him so the neharbeyheem could be placed into the asuk.

13 We were told by Hosek that under no circumstances were we to cause direct harm to the Akamu without clearing it with him first.

14 Otherwise we should just wait for the neharbeyheem to be released upon their maveth.

15 I asked Yago if he knew what a maveth was exactly. He said he heard others say it was something to do with zehman. Of course he thought it was some sort of punishment put upon the Akamu based on what he saw them doing to each other. I sort of agreed that not even the Achim or Uri would act as the Akamu were. Clearly the fixes of bachar and chalal were not really working.

16 I was out in the vacant lands of the Tsaatsium Erets with Yago one day when we got an urgent message from Hosek for all the Achim to return to the Kli.

17 Hosek ordered the Kli off the Tsaatsium Erets as fast as possible. As we were leaving the Tsaatsium Erets the Kli was hit hard by a wave.

18 The whole of the Tsaatsium Erets was returning to its original state of the chaos of the Toho Erets.

Chapter 6

Ursprung der Unanständigkeit

(The Origin of Indecency)

The Origin of Indecency, this is the curse laid upon Canaan, son of Ham for seeing Noah's nakedness. It is interesting how the section opens up with references to what would technically be an earlier part of Genesis dealing with the clothing of Adam and Eve. This is also the first time the text is making direct references to names mentioned in canonical texts, but it is interesting how it still maintains the writing style of prefacing the names of people with what kind of person they are (i.e. Good human vs. bad human). It is clear that this is to show some sort of purposeful division not just between the spirits and the material world, and also the individual kinds of material creatures.

1 Early on, the Akamu attempted to cover up their ervah with the use of chagowr, but Adonai sent forth the Uri to teach the Akamu to make or-kuttoneth.

2 We Achim simple watched and waited for each Akamu's neharbeyheem to be released. But now there was no covering that would help the Akamu, for Adonai has reversed his decision to make the Akamu.

3 The Kli settled on the surface of the Toho Erets that was reformed.

4 We were sinking due to the damage to the hull, and all of the crew worked with great efforts to stem the flooding. Even Hosek could be seen working feverishly to stop the flooding.

5 I was detecting the presence of another craft in the Toho Erets. It appeared to have Akamu on it. But I thought all of them had perished.

6 Hosek had discovered that the Uri were sent to help one of the Akamu before the flood.

7 An Akamu who found favor with Adonai.

8 The Kli came to rest finally, and the Toho Erets once more had turned into the Tsaatsuim Erets.

9 Hosek ordered the Achim out of the Kli to make further repairs. The hull damage was extensive.

10 It was clear that return to the Onyia was not going to happen. Worse we could no longer communicate with the Onyia or the Tower as the array was smashed upon the Kli coming to rest.

11 The Tsaatsuim Erets was bare. Hosek choose me and Yago to go explore and see what was available for repairs.

12 One day Yago and I came upon the Akamu craft built by the Uri.

13 The Akamu had abandon the craft, but the smell was horrible. The Akamu had made a mess of the place.

14 We scavenged what parts we could use and returned to the Kli.

15 Hosek ordered both Yago and I to go out once more and look for the Akamu. He wanted us to observe them and follow them, but not to harm them.

16 After some time, Yago and I found the Akamu who survived. They appeared to be attempting to contact the Tower with some primitive form of communication.

17 To our surprise there was a response from the Tower. The Tower called the Akamu by a new name- Adriel.

18 The one working the communication device was known as Adriel Noah.

19 Yago had become bored watching the Adriel Noah and the other Adriels.

20 While the Tower had given them a new name, to Yago and I, they seemed no different than the Akamu before.

21 Yago whispered to me a crazy idea of playing a joke upon the Adriel Noah as a way to break up the boredom.

22 We would inspire him to make shekar and see what happens.

23 I questioned Yago about this idea of his. But he assured me that no harm would come to the Adriels from it. At least the harm that Hosek spoke of.

24 Although once more I questioned Yago and said clearly to him that in inspiring them thusly will bring harm to some and surly he could see that.

25 He agreed with the vision, but again he insisted that it was not the harm Hosek meant. Hosek clearly didn't want the Adriels to lose their neharbeyheem by our hands without Hosek's permission.

26 I agreed and so we inspired the Adriel Noah to make the shekar. We both agreed not to mention this to Hosek or any of the other Achim.

27 Yago and I watched as the Adriel Noah started to act even odder than before upon consuming the shekar. Clearly the shekar produced an unusual reaction with the Adriels, unlike what we Achim would experience.

28 At one point the Adriel Noah exposed his ervah, and then Yago inspired the Adriel Ham to look upon Adriel Noah's ervah.

29 I pulled Yago away before he continued to inspire more Adriels to come see the ervah of the Adriel Noah. I did so because I could see this was clearly going against Hosek's orders.

30 Two of the Adriels came and placed a covering over the Adriel Noah. Later when Adriel Noah had recovered from the effects of the shekar, he uttered a curse upon the children of Adriel Ham calling them Akamu once more.

31 I told Yago that what he has done cannot be undone. Hosek will be mad at us for disobeying his orders. Yago didn't really seem to care too much as he was laughing too hard at the whole vision of what was to come to the cursed Akamu. He assured me that Hosek would be pleased, and I should not worry so much about the vision of what is to come because of his actions.

32 So we returned after some time, and reported nothing of this to Hosek or the other Achim.

Chapter 7

Jakob und der Gefallenen

(Jacob and the Fallen)

For this section of text there are no notes by von Hemrick. As such I have had to translate this using the matrix first into German then into English. It seems to be recalling the section of Genesis dealing with Jacob being re-named Israel (although the re-naming part is missing from the passage).

This part is dealing with an older folklore style of the passage than what is in Genesis currently. I think the passage represents an encouragement to readers to fight or wrestle with one's material demons in order to obtain spiritual enlightenment. It also shows that while we may have a firm grasp on our faults, sometimes this is temporary or even greater evils could befall us on our journey later.

1 One evening Hosek went off by himself. I could see him in the distance talking to someone, but could not make him out. Later Hosek returned and had a mission for me.

2 Hosek had learned that the Uri had been sent to aid an Adriel named Jacob. Adriel Jacob was on a journey to meet his brother, and I was to intercept him at the river. I was not to let him pass and use any means at my disposal to stop him. Hosek was very firm with this order.

3 I set forth and found the Adriel Jacob attempting to cross the river at a low point. I quickly grabbed him, and we wrestled in the water.

4 For an Adriel he was pretty agile against my form. All night we fought and I could tell he was weakening. I could see the vison of drowning him in the river by my hands, but also him escaping my grasp.

5 I managed to hit Adriel Jacob in the hip pulling the leg from the socket. I knew I had him at this point, but somehow he managed to best me.

6 I could see in the distance Uri coming toward the river. Their armor glowed like the morning sun.

7 The Adriel Jacob had a firm grip on me. He pressed me for my name. I refused, but his grip grew tighter against me.

8 I had no choice but to free myself and escape before the Uri met up with us. So I made a bargain with the Adriel Jacob. I would allow him to pass unharmed if he freed me, and I would give him my name so his kind could have power over the Achim. But I told him that this power would be temporary and that there are Achim greater than I that could still over power his kind. The Adriel Jacob agreed and released me. I fled for a time into the sandy wastes to hide from the Uri and Hosek.

Chapter 8

Gebogenen Stange Völker

(Bent Pole Peoples)

Recently I came across a passage that seems to elaborate on the biblical reference in Genesis concerning Onan (although von Hemrick's notes seem to concentrate more on a group of people mentioned in the passage).

The story of Onan is but 5 lines in the Bible, but historically this passage from Pope Leo IX in 1054 forward has been referenced significantly over time by the Church (mostly in the 20th Century). Although Zuriel's text seems to concentrate on a foreshadowing of the future, the issues of sexual problems associated with mixed marriages, (i.e. Judah's marriage to a Canaanite woman) and the ancient Jewish legal traditions of the firstborn's lineage and inheritance.

I do recall reading somewhere that one scholar thought while the sexual crime committed by Onan is clearly documented, that the reason God killed Onan was the law he violated was the first command given to the human race of multiplying. In short, Onan paid lip service to God's law and thus did not allow God's will for human salvation to be transmitted through the human race.

1 One day while near the Akamu's village of Achzib, Hosek called me to him. He wanted me to hear of a mission I was to undertake.

2 "Listen, Zuriel and say nothing." Hosek instructed me. Hosek placed upon a rock a small device of some kind. It began to project a shadowy image.

3 Then the shadowy image spoke the following to me, "Zuriel, you will go to the house of the Adriel Judah, and there you will incite his first born to defile his mother Shua. Adonai will kill him for such a crime, and next you will incite his father to press Adonai's will upon his second son Onan. Onan is weak of heart being more Akamu than Adriel, so then you may easily enter him and guide him to take Adonai's will into his own hands. All of this is important so that it will be remembered by the Adriel. In this way many of them will perish by the hands of the Dorak Stauros Loas who will conquer the world at our bidding."

4 The image faded, and Hosek put the device away. I asked Hosek who was that I saw. But Hosek said to me that it is best not to ask, for if I did I would not like what I see. It will only confirm my vision of the nothingness.

5 Hosek took me aside and told me, that there will come a time when the Uri will track us down and bind us. But we will gather forces from the Akamu to challenge the Uri and defeat the Adriel who they guide. This is what was meant by the Dorak Stauros Loas. These are the people who will be part of our forces.

6 I did as I was instructed and most assuredly I watched Adonai remove the neharbeyheem from the Adriel Judah's first born, as well as the second son Onan. I easily captured both neharbeyheems and took them to Hosek who placed them into the asuk which placed them into the Tehom.

Chapter 9

Ehe von Mann

(Marriage of Man)

von Hemrick called this the Marriage of Man. The writer is elaborating on the institution of marriage and trying to show the differences between two kinds of marriage. You can sort of tell the gnostic like tone of the piece in how marriage is treated

.

1 Hosek called me in after the Akim had made the changes to the Dabar to discuss our mission.

2 "Zuriel, you are my most steadfast follower despite the vision you see, an unbreakable trusting stone. We have been given a long term mission dealing with the Akamu. We are to help the Akamu with caring for the Tsaatsuim Erets. To accomplish this, we will need to give them certain knowledge to help them. This is where you and the other Achim will play a critical role."

3 "You will instruct the other Achim to provide the Akamu chathan and Akamu ishshah with the knowledge of the tsaphad. They are not to know of the berith ownah."

4 "It is very important that all the Akamu know of the way of the tsaphad. It is the only way the chalal can be fulfilled. In time the Akamu will come to see the way of the tsaphad as a better way. They will come to realize that chalaq and karath will be possible with the way of the

tsaphad. It will be important to us later when the Navakalesen arise from the Akamu."

5 I asked Hosek, "What is the chalal? And why do the Akamu need to know of the tsaphad for no Achim needed either the tsaphad or berith ownah."

6 Hosek replied, "Chalal was needed to correct a defect in the Akamu. It is something special from Adonai. But we must teach the Akamu of the ways of the tsaphad, so it must be fulfilled. For such knowledge will ensure that they never reach a certain spiritual understanding. This is the purpose of the chalal, to ensure that spiritual understanding is not achieved. If they knew of the berith ownah, then it is possible that they will come to understand more than they were meant to understand. This is all you need to know at this time."

7 So I left Hosek and began to instruct the other Achim of the plan. The tsaphad was adopted very quickly by the Akamu and came with it chalaq and karath.

Chapter 10

Gesicht Gottes

(Face of God)

I am not certain why von Hemrick calls this section the Face of God, but as far as I can tell, it seems to be referring to sections of the Book of Revelations despite referring to the Book of Job. This would indicate the possibility that the writer is trying to elaborate on those elements in the Book of Revelations through the use of the Book of Job and thus tying the old and new together creating greater justification for the new text.

This section seems to go into great pains to reveal hidden meanings and thoughts concerning certain realities associated with human sexuality, the nature of conflict between God and the Satan, the material world and the spiritual world, and pretty much any other "secret" understanding the writer could throw into the text.

Reisen Sie zurück in den Himmel

(Travel Back to Heaven)

1 After much work, the Kli was finally repaired and the time of Yatsab had come, Hosek wished to return to the Panim of Adonai to give an account of what had occurred with the mission.

2 Hosek gave the order for all the Achim to return to the Kli, and we left the Tsaatsuim Erets for the Oniya.

3 The great wind that was above the Tsaatsium Erets appeared to be no more, and we easily could approach the Onyia and the Tower.

4 As we approached the Onyia, I could tell much had changed since our departure.

5 It appeared to me that the Uri had been making some modifications to the Onyia. It was as if they were preparing for some sort of battle.

6 While the darkness to which I first knew surrounded all of the Onyia, the Onyia and all aboard shown with a great light.

7 So radiant was this light that my head began to hurt with its brilliance, and it became difficult to dock with the Onyia.

8 Upon docking with the Onyia, Hosek gave orders to resupply the Kli and make any additional repairs while he went to the Panim of Adonai. But Hosek took me aside and asked me to accompany him.

9 Hosek said to me, "Zuriel, there is secret knowledge in the Tower that we need for our mission. So I need you to make your way to that secret knowledge and reveal it to me after the Yatsab."

10 I asked Hosek how I was to obtain this knowledge since I was not a Uri.

11 He said to me, "Here take this maphteach it will allow you to easily get past any Uri that questions your presence."

Dichtungen, Trompeten und Schalen

(Seals, Trumpets and Bowls)

This section of the translations expands the first part of the Book of Job where there is a conversation between the Satan and God concerning the state of Job's devotion to God. But in this version the author has clearly tied in parts of the Book of Revelations as well, which is very interesting because most of the Book of Revelations tends to tie into other books like Daniel, Isaiah, Jeremiah and Ezekiel. In fact, there are phrases like "a year, two years, and half year" (Rev. 12:14) which ties back to the phrase "a time, two times, and half a time" (Dan. 7:25). This is not to say that the Book of Revelations was simply a re-hashing of old texts into some cryptic format, but one could say about all the books in the Bible, the Book of Revelations is by far the closest we get to a gnostic text in the sense of secret knowledge hidden in written words.

So much has been written on and from the Book of Revelations concerning the end times it is clear that one thing is for certain- we humans, like the fallen angel in this translation, really want to know the outcome of events as far in advance as possible. Imagine what one can do if you knew the winning lottery numbers for the big jackpot in advance, or even better imagine knowing exactly the date and place of your own death? How much effort would you put into changing those events?

12 Hosek took his place at the Yatsab before the Panim of Adonai in the Tower, but was questioned by Adonai from where he came.

13 Hosek said, "I come from Tsaatsuim Erets. I have wondered upon its surface and have found the Akamu to be in a state of tame before you Adonai."

14 Adonai responded, "Are you sure? Even those known as Adriel?"

15 "Yes", Hosek said, "even the Adriel who were to be in a state of zakah before you."

16 "Even the Adriel Job, my servant? Clearly he is in such a state of zakah that he glows like the Uri." said Adonai.

17 Hosek responded, "Even the Adriel Job is flawed in such a way that his state of zakah can be easily turned into tame."

18 "Are you so sure?" questioned Adonai.

19 At this point the others present at the Yatsab were becoming indignant by Hosek's presence and line of questioning before Adonai, and they began to murmur amongst themselves.

20 Before Hosek had time to answer, Adonai silenced the room and spoke these words, "Hosek, since you are so sure of yourself concerning the state of the Akamu and Adriel, and because you are the first among the Akim, I shall grant you control over the first four Beriths."

21 At which point the one known as Adonai's Omer came before the Panim of Adonai and broke before Hosek the four Beriths; one of white, one of red, one of black and one of pale."

22 I did as Hosek had asked and upon the end of the first day of the Yatsab I came to him and spoke these words, "My leader Hosek, you have been given the first four of seven Beriths. The remaining three are for the one known as Adonai's Omer. The one the Adriel will call Yasha Erets Am. They are the prequel to events concerning Adonai's Omer and his rise to power."

23 Upon the second day of the Yatsab, Hosek took his place before the Panim of Adonai with

the others. And again Adonai questioned Hosek to why he was present.

24 Hosek responded, "Adonai I am concerned about the Tsaatsuim Erets and its fate. My brothers and I cannot see like you, and it deeply concerns us."

25 Adonai asked, "And what do you want?"

26 Hosek responded, "Is it not possible for you to fix the events of the Tsaatsuim Erets so we may know of them?"

27 "What you say is possible", said Adonai.

28 Hosek continued, "If it pleases Adonai, it would be most helpful to all present that such a thing be done."

29 At which point the others present broke out again in a mummer amongst themselves, and again Adonai silenced them all.

30 Adonai spoke these words concerning the Tsaatsuim Erets, "I will fix the end of the Tsaatsuim Erets so you all may see it. You will know it because I have set forth events that will take place in an order that I shall reveal to you all."

31 Again I did as Hosek had asked and upon the end of the second day of the Yatsab I came to him and spoke these words, "My leader Hosek, I have learned the hidden knowledge that has now become revealed. After the Beriths will be the Taqoa in which the one known as Adonai's Omer will announce his coming. Many of the Akamu will die upon the coming of the Taqoa."

32 Upon the third day and final day of the Yatsab, Hosek took his place before the Panim of Adonai with the others, and once more Adonai questioned Hosek's presence.

33 Hosek responded, "Adonai I am still troubled by the Tsaatsuim Erets and its fate. Since my brothers and I roam the Tsaatsuim Erets, clearly it would be most helpful if we could do more than just see its fate."

34 Adonai responded, "What you ask can be given but only for small period of time. What I have put into motion I will not change concerning thc Tsaatsuim Erets for clearly you can see this."

35 "Why yes Adonai I can see that things are now fixed, and if it pleases Adonai I would like my request honored as the first among the Akim", responded Hosek.

36 At which point the assembly present broke out in an uproar at such a request. They were all indignant at Hosek for such presumption before Adonai.

37 Adonai silenced them all and spoke these words, "Hosek, you are truly the first amongst the Akim and you will be remembered by all for being first, and because of this I will grant you your desire but be warned that what I have put into motion cannot be changed for I will not go back on my word. The Tsaatsuim Erets will not last forever."

38 Upon the end of the third day of Yatsab, I saw Hosek and spoke these words to him, "My leader Hosek, this is all I have found concerning what is to come. The one known as Adonai's Omer will cause a war to happen between all. Adonai's Omer will ask the Bethulah to come to the Tsaatsuim Erets to fight in the war. She will warn the Akamu and Adriel alike of the time of Qetsaph in which all of Tsaatsuim Erets will be destroyed. After the time of Qetsaph there will only be the Onyia and the Tower, and they will leave all behind for Chadash."

39 Hosek said the following to me, "My faithful Zuriel, you have done well on this mission. And much has been learned and granted to us."

Das Wahrsagen des Christus und der Krieg

(The Foretelling of the Christ and the War)

These passages seem to be an interesting point of view concerning the Messiah or the Christ. It is written in a way that would support the standard Gnostic view of the Christ being trapped in human form, and yet it also has some other elements to it. What is more interesting is that it is a conversation from the other side's perspective as it were, which is unique.

40 I came before Hosek and asked him to tell me of the one the Uri call 'Adonai's Omer' or what the Adriel call 'Yasha Erets Am'. And this is what he said,

41 "Zuriel, I tell you these things as a warning to tell to all the other Achim. The one known as 'Adonai's Omer' or 'Yasha Erets Am' is to be feared by our kind for he will end everything. He will bring about a war against all and nothing will be spared against his wrath."

42 "There will be some of the Adriel who will seek him as an eternal malak and kohen; the builder of Adonai's bayith and hekal for them."

43 "But I tell you he will come down through Adonai's neshama-nur to the Tsaatsuim Erets to be among the Adriel and the Akamu, and that it is then we will test him and put him on trial."

44 "Even though he is the mashach of the Adriel, he will be like them at that point and powerless. His rauch will be trapped desiring nothing but release to return to the Tower."

45 "Once he returns to the Tower the war will continue until the end. That end you see is the nothingness; the nothingness that will be brought upon all because of Adonai's Omer."

46 "While our rauch cannot be destroyed here by those of the Tsaatsium Erets, all Achim are not eternal. Not even the Uri are eternal. Once we were promised this, but Adonai has revoked that promise and in his place put Adonai's Omer."

47 "This is why Adonai's Omer will wage a war against us. He will ensure that the revocation of that promise is carried out even at the expense of all of creation."

48 "But this I will say to you, not everything foretold will come to pass. The war will be long and the battles will be many."

49 "Go Zuriel, tell the others to be ready for war."

Ende der Menschheit

(The End of Humanity)

This piece is featured rather prominently in von Hemrick's notes. von Hemrick's notes are concerned with the various studies about eugenics of his time and the issues being raised by the texts concerning the creation of what is called the Zoons. It appears in his notes that he is trying to link the two ideas into one universal idea, but the text itself seems more concerned with foreshadowing of future events with humanity and how the Satan plans to destroy humanity.

50 Hosek called me to him to give me instruction on what is to come with the war.

51 "Listen very carefully, Zuriel" Hosek said, "what I am about to tell you are of things to come and concern the plans involving Adoani's Omer."

52 Hosek continued, "All the Adriel follow the ways of Adoani when it comes to zanah, but not the Akamu." I was not familiar with zanah or what it meant.

53 Hosek continued again, "All you need to know is that it is through zanah that Adoani allows both Adriel and Akamu to continue his work. And it is important that zanah should follow a certain way so the plans of Adoani's Omer will come to pass, and the end of everything will occur."

54 "But we can end this all through a series of careful steps," Hosek said.

55 Hosek told me that since the creation of the first Akamu they were made to be echad-neged-azar to each other.

56 But this has not worked out despite attempts to correct the problem through the addition of chalal and zehman.

57 Both Akamu and Adriel will suffer with the problem of zanah, and it will cause them both grief and joy.

58 Although now with the pending war, the zanah will be our weapon according to Hosek.

59 Hosek then said, "In the time of dal we will give both Akamu and Adriel alike the knowledge of the zamam. With this knowledge will come in the following order: dalah, dar, dothan, darqon, and hege. Once these are done there will be a great repression against Adoani's Omer and it will happen mostly in the lands of the Navakalesen. By the time of hayyah we will strike with such a force that a great exodus will begin away from Adoani's Omer. A great maschith will befall upon them, and many will become halak-maveth-neharbeyheem. Oh, how we will celebrate during that time, but it will be short lived until the cheva-paal is given to the Akamu. Once the Akamu have this, they will build for us the eternal zoons. That is when the true battle will begin, and the Akamu and Adriel both will be no more."

60 I told Hosek I have seen the great maschith he speaks of and asked if it was to be during the time of zoth.

61 But he told me that it was not for that time, and the time of zoth is reserved to the Bethulah to speak of and is not for us to control.

62 Instead he told me the great maschith will be unseen to all the Akamu and Adriel, but they will know of it and the kohen of the Adriel will be saddened.

63 It will be the result of a great battle between the Uri and Achim, and strike at their very hearts.

Chapter 11

Wächter Vogel

(The Guardian Bird)

This part of the text seems to tie into parts of the Old Testament where typically an Angel of the Lord is used to kill humans, such as 2 Kings 19:35 where the Assyrians are killed during the night. According to von Hemrick's notes, he supposes what is meant "by the envy of the Devil" in the Book of Wisdom 2:24 is more that of the joy of being the recipient of human souls and thus the bringer of death. The Greek word used for "envy" in the original text is "phthonos" which can mean "being happy for the misfortune of others" as well as having a "grudge". Historically St. Augustine and St. Dominic have viewed the sin of the Satan as being pure pride and envy. Between this section and previous sections, the author Zuriel is offering the docetae view that those "fallen angels" are first and foremost unable to understand the will of God and thus reject it because they cannot understand it, and secondly Hosek (to whom I believe is the Satan) clearly has his own mission and operates on his own terms. If the Satan is doing these things out of pride or envy, this has yet to be fully explained by these texts, although a possible motive may have been given in the translation entitled "The Foretelling of the Christ and the War" where Hosek (i.e. the Satan) explains that all angels (both fallen and not) were to have eternal life where they go to the next world but were denied it and given only immortal life instead which ends with this world.

1 For some time Hosek had ordered the Achim to go forth among the Akamu and teach them how their lives were meaningless. No one would come back from the Tehom, and all were food for the Tsale.

2 As a result, many Akamu realized that it was far better to live with a joyful zest and make

use of all that creation offers in the shortness of their lives.

3 It came to pass though that our teachings were noticed by the Tower through the Uri, and they sent forth an emissary with a message to Hosek.

4 "I have come to deliver this message to you in person", said the brightly cladded Uri as she handed a small stone to Hosek.

5 Hosek took the stone and retired to his room for a brief moment only to burst forth saying, "Strip the armor from this Guardian Uri and throw her in a cell."

6 Hosek then ordered Asmodeus to go forth to the desert lands of the Akamu to the east and inspire a deep fear in their kings of the Adriel kingdoms of the west; a fear so deep that it will cause a dispersion of the Adriel forever.

7 And so Asmodeus did as he as commanded, and the Akamu began to wage war against the Adriel kingdoms.

8 As before, Hosek ordered all the Achim to collect the neharbeyheem from both the Akamu and Adriel alike and bring them to him to be placed in the asuk as the battles took place.

9 But as the Akamu made their advance upon the Adriel city of Yerushalem, a multitude of Uri flew down from Onyia.

10 In their lead was Elisheva who I had not seen since the time of choice.

11 Before the sun had set, and the Akamu prepared for night, Elisheva met with Hosek to discuss terms.

12 Hosek ordered me to return to the Kli and release the Guardian Uri kept there, and give her back her armor.

13 I arrived at the cell blocks of the Kli and opened the one with the Guardian Uri.

14 "I know my fellow Uri are here," she said and then continued, "You really cannot see what is going on here can you? You do not know what this is all about do you?"

15 "All I know is I am here to release you and give you back your armor"; I told her tossing her glowing armor at her.

16 As she put on her armor she commented once more, "Are all your kind truly blind to the ways of Adonai?"

17 I had no idea what she was talking about for the ways of Adonai to me were nothing but pure chaos as it was for all Achim.

18 I walked with her back to where Hosek and Elisheva were, and by this point the sun had set.

19 Elisheva pulled the Guardian Uri aside and spoke to her in private and she gave a brief glance back in our direction then out towards the Akamu camps. She took from Elisheva a sword and drew it above her head and from its blade issued forth a blue white flame.

20 I immediately recognized her as the one who took the first born in the lands of the Akamu kingdom of Matsor.

21 She then preceded towards the Akamu camps with extreme haste, and as she whizzed by me she said to me "I am Aya, and your days are numbered Achim."

22 Hosek then yelled out orders for all the Achim to go forth and bring him the Akamu's neharbeyheems.

Icon - The Good Angel Aya, Chapter 11, Line 21

Chapter 12

Amerikas Zerstörung

(America's Destruction)

In von Hemrick's notes, he believes he sees the key to how the United States will fall in the war, although he does not specify what that is exactly and it seems he does not make his beliefs known to the commanding powers. Personally the translation appears to me to be two biblical elements put together to form some sort of prophetic message. Part of it appears to be from 2 Kings 9:27 and from Isaiah 24. Most of it appears to be a personal reflection, and I have no idea how von Hemrick gets the idea of this passage that America will be destroyed.

While I will give von Hemrick the benefit of the doubt concerning the fact that the transliterated word for America is used in the text, I have not a clue to whom this "Gur" person is exactly and von Hemrick's notes don't mention who he thinks he is either. As an American reading this passage to me it reads that the Satan created George Washington (a.k.a. The Father of the Nation), which would be totally odd and weird. While I know George Washington was a Mason, and there is history in this country on issues with Masons (to the point that there was a political movement to remove Masons from every office and seat of power in the United States), I really don't think George Washington is the son of the Satan.

Whoever this "Gur" person is- 1. I don't think it's George Washington because that makes no sense with due consideration of von Hemrick's notes thinking he will allow Germany to win the war, 2. It is clearly referring to any other person whose children (i.e. Americans) will give the priests of the followers of God living in America troublous or at least make them always sad, and 3. We must not forget who is making this prophetic claim to do something (i.e. The Satan) and as such while his power is great (as mentioned in the translation) it is not boundless and there are other forces at play that will no doubt foil his plans.

1 Yago and I were ordered to go to tempt the Adriel Athaliah through dreams so as to inspire her son Adriel Ahaziah to change the ways of the Adriel.

2 Our mission was a success, and soon new ways were being introduced.

3 But evidently this came to the notice of the Uri who became very offended by what we had done.

4 The Uri inspired some of the Adriel to find fault with the Adriel Ahaziah and so they hunted him down.

5 Yago and I reported all this to Hosek who became indignant over the situation.

6 Hosek said, "For this action we will raise up one who will be named Gur from where the Adriel Ahaziah was wounded, and he shall become the father of the Navakalesen. It is from his seed that all I have said before will come to pass. The kohen of the Adriel living in those lands will eternally be saddened."

7 Hosek's words came to be known to the Tower. It became known to all the Achim that there were plans for once more to destroy Tsaatsuim Erets and return it to Toho Erets.

8 There were also plans being prepared by Adonai's Omer for a place where all the Achim will be imprisoned.

9 While we could easily see all this and that some of us will manage to escape these things, none of the Achim could escape the vision of nothingness that was its conclusion.

10 I could not help but ponder the nothingness.

11 The bitterness of the nothingness, the first thing I saw as absolute truth.

12 "How could all that Adonai made end up in nothingness?" I asked myself.

13 Hosek was right, we have made our bachar, and it was correct.

14 Even so, at times a rage would build in me because of the nothingness I saw and then the bitterness would grab me again.

15 Yago once told me the nothingness filled him with total rage; all he could do was go out and frighten the young Adriels and Akamus he would come upon.

16 Although I never saw such things from Hosek, for he was the first of the Achim and had so much power and might about him.

17 To me he gleamed like a thousand gems shining in the morning sun.

18 Hosek was right about our bachar, and he is correct about these things.

19 For he tells us not to worry about the nothingness, for it will come to pass, and there is something better to come.

die Hexe

(The Witch)

von Hemrick has a personal reflection about some sort of the bullying incident in his days as a youth at college involving what is known in German as die Hexe or the Witch. A nocturnal witch comes to torture young men at night by sitting on their chests. This sounds like the medical condition known as chest-sleep paralysis (my uncle Bert used to suffer from this issue). von Hemrick's notes go on to bitterly complain about those who bullied him, and at the same time, in vengeful spite, he seems to hope the demonic entity mentioned in the translations will seek them out as much as the Satan plans to send forth this entity to torture the followers of God.

The entity being mentioned in the text is one of the oldest mentioned in the Bible and has been talked of in literature for a long time. The name of this entity is mentioned in Isaiah 34:14, and extensively in Medieval Jewish Kabalistic traditions and other similar texts. Her name in the Book of Zuriel is Lel, but she is also known as Lilith (a.k.a. The female night demon or female demon thought to roam the deserts).

In the Alphabet of Ben Sira (a Jewish pseudoepigraphical text from sometime around 700 to 1000 CE), the text goes into length to explain why in Genesis, there are apparently two women created. In one part of Genesis you have God is making man and woman, and then later you read how Eve is taken from Adam's side. So as the Ben Sira tradition goes that first woman created was Lilith who became a demon or succubus because she wanted to dominate the male-female relationship and Adam refused. In the Book of Zuriel though it seems that Lel, as she is known, is related more to the creatures known as the Nephilim in Genesis 6:1-4 who had evidently gone awry and now have become servants of the Satan.

There is a growing cold war between the "Good Angels" and "Bad Angels" as we seem to be marching towards the coming of the Christ and with each incident provoking a future prophetic prediction of how the Satan plans to seek revenge for each act against him, like some sort of evil character in a cheap cartoon revealing his evil plans. This particular incident seems to come out of the Book of Daniel, one of the earliest known apocalyptic styles of writings in the Bible, and one heavily attributed to early prophesy of the coming of Christ and His kingdom. Elements of the Book of Revelations also seem to appear mixed in as well.

I have also found out from my friend Alyssa, that apparently this particular translation seems to heavily rely on a common but old form of cryptology known as Gematria. Alyssa also suspects that some of the date words mentioned in a previous passage might be some form of Gematria in reverse. You see Gematria in the Book of Revelations concerning the number of the Beast. I wish I could solve these math problems, but this is not my area, and I leave it to others to figure them out.

1 Hosek had assigned a good portion of the Achim to the Akamu lands of the east where we were to watch the Adriels who were being held there by the Akamu people living there.

2 One day, Yago and I noticed a single Uri go into the chambers of the Akamu Nebuchadnezzar.

3 The Uri used a seal upon the room so that we could not enter to see what the Uri was doing. We discovered later that a dream was given to the Akamu Nebuchadnezzar which tortured him greatly.

4 Word came to us that other Uri were about the Akamu city as well, and seemed very interested in the Adriel Daniel and his companions.

5 Soon enough it came to be the Uri's plan unfolded and the Adriel Daniel and his

companions had risen to a position of power within the lands of the Akamu Nebuchadnezzar.

6 Asmodeus, who was in charge of this campaign, was greatly distressed by these events and was given. Commands by Hosek to see to it that the Adriels lose their seat of power.

7 So Asmodeus ordered us to inspire fear among the Akamu concerning the Adriel and cause the Akamu Nebuchadnezzar to make a new god for all the people to worship by penalty of burning.

8 Soon enough our trap had been sprung. The Adriels refused to worship the new god, and the companions of the Adriel Daniel were to be sentenced to burned.

9 Many Achim gathered to watch the building of the furnace so as to capture the neharbeyheem of the Adriels to be thrown in.

10 But when it came to the companions of the Adriel Daniel, I noticed a Guardian Uri in their midst standing with them in the flames of the furnace.

11 She drew her sword, and blue white flame issued forth.

12 She began to swing the sword around her head in such a manner that the flames did not touch the companions of the Adriel Daniel.

13 It was then I realized it was the Guardian Uri I had seen earlier, the one known as Aya.

14 But before I could warn my fellow Achim, a host of Guardian Uri descended upon all the Achim gathered, forcing us to scatter.

15 Later it became known to us that the Akamu Nebuchadnezzar changed his ways concerning the Adriels in his lands. With this news Asmodeus became distressed and sent me to Hosek to report all that had taken place.

16 Upon reporting all that had occurred in the lands of the Akamu Nebuchadnezzar, Hosek became enraged and said the following,

17 "For this these actions by the Uri, I will unbind in the desert the cheva Lel; One of many from the union of the Akim with Akamu ibriy who the Akim left behind, and that I have bound for my use. But it will take time for the cheva Lel to gather her strength for she has been weakened by her bindings, but during Hayyah she will be known as the relentless one. The one who will cause many Adriels who are mishchah to no longer listen to the Kohen of the Adriels, for she will press upon even the Kohen to poison the very Edah of Omer. The poison mentioned by the Kohen whose number is 1478. Not even the great prophet, whose number is 1560, will be able to stop her. And it will be too late by the time the one whose number is 180 reveals her to the people of the Navakalesen. How I will laugh during those times for the traps I will lay because of the cheva Lel. Those who think they are doing righteous deeds will fall for the traps she will lay for me only to be seen as self-righteous instead. With our help we will teach the Akamu and Adriel the ways of the furnace so by the time of Hayyah both the Akamu ishshah and Adriel ishshah will want to be free of their bondage caused by the cheva Lel and the ways of the furnace, for no longer will they feel that they are truly echad-neged-azar."

18 I could see all that Hosek said will come true during Hayyah.

19 I could not shake the vision of the nothingness that stood before me.

20 My spirit's heart was heavy with the knowledge of the nothingness and my spirit's mind could not figure a way out of the nothingness that is to come.

21 All this distressed me greatly. All I wanted was to see all that Hosek said of Hayyah to come true now, but I knew it was for later.

Chapter 14

Weisheit

(Wisdom)

It is a fascinating section which was added to the text by a later author. This is not an uncommon practice. Usually when this occurs, it is because of a part of the text was added later or had another author complete it or was combined with some other unassociated text.

This particular passage pulls from Proverbs 8 dealing with the discussion on Wisdom, but in this case there seems to be something more sinister in mind including once more writings alluding to possible future events. This also may be an attempt to water-down or make more acceptable the developing idea of the Sophia myth common in some Gnostic traditions. It could be a simple rejection of that notion and acceptance of more traditional understandings of Wisdom from Jewish literature. I suspect based on the current trend of the text that it might be more of the latter.

What is interesting is the conversation between Hosek and Zuriel concerning the "wisdom" of certain actions and the nature of the material-spiritual worlds. It is possible these early Gnostic writers are trying to show the reason why the material world is "evil" which is a common theme in Gnosticism, known as Manichaeism. Manichaeism was totally outlawed by Emperor Theodosius the First in 382 despite surviving somewhere between the 3rd and 7th centuries before finally dying out. The idea today is not accepted simply by the fact in Genesis 1:31 you find the statement "God looked at everything he had made, and found it very good" and with any sense of logic if the material world is evil then why would God would call it good? This text seems to support the Genesis 1:31 notion of the material world being inherently good, and that an evil entity (i.e. the Satan) is responsible for the distortions.

1 Hosek called to me one day and asked me to walk with him. As I did, he told me the following,

2 "Listen very well Zuriel, there is one known as Chokmah. She is a spirit of old, before you and me. She was here before all of creation, but she was made by Adonai. She is to us an eternal one for she rests with Adonai. She was Adonai's artisan for all of the Tsaatsuim Erets, and provided to the first Akamu her fruits of her designs. Even today she continues to provide both Akamu and Adriel both the fruits of her designs. In the beginning I tried to capture her as she played with the Akamu, but instead she laid a trap for me instead. A trap I will free myself from, and ruin her designs by making it my own. And so I have a plan to make her fruit very bitter to both the Akamu and Adriel. Listen well, Zuriel to what I am about to say."

3 Hosek continued as I sat upon a nearby rock, "Chokmah not only provides counsel to the Akamu and Adriel, but she follows Adonai's Omer and the one known as the Sahed. Before dalah, we will begin to close the ears of the Akamu and even the Adriel to her counsel and turn their neharbeyheem's heart to stone."

4 I asked how we were to do this great feat. Hosek responded, "We will instruct some of the Akamu and Adriel of certain knowledge; a kind of knowledge that Chokmah has kept from them on purpose. This knowledge will make them forget about spiritual things and only look towards the things of the Tsaatsuim Erets designed by Chokmah. They will become so grounded and obsessed with the discovery of the designs of the Tsaatsuim Erets that they will forget who was the designer or Adonai its

creator. The counsel she used to provide will be replaced with a cold stony way that only considers the knowledge of what they can see, taste, smell and feel. For every time the Kohen of the Adriel mention the counsel of Chokmah to all willing to hear, they will be ridiculed as being fools and followers of nonsense. Even Adonai's Omer will be rejected and his feats will be considered impossible by the designs. Those that listen to us will see the counsel of Chokmah nothing more than just another thought with no weight upon the scales to that of any other thought, and what we have taught will be seen has pure gold tipping those scales to our designs.'

5 I dared to interrupt Hosek, "but if we give the Akamu and Adriel this knowledge so they forget about spiritual things, will they not forget about us as well? How will all the rest then come to pass if they will not even listen to us?"

6 Hosek responded, "Zuriel, while it is true they will forget of spiritual things they will not forget how to listen to the Achim. For we will perform wondrous feats and entice their imaginations with thoughts that will keep them following us, for they will think it is all part of the designs of Chokmah."

7 Again I dared to ask another question, "but will not the Uri do the same as us?"

8 Hosek responded, "Oh Zuriel, you should trust your vision more for you know all that I have said will come to pass for you can see it as much as I. And while it is true the Uri will try to undue all our plans, but as dalah, dar, dothan, darqon, and hege unfold they will be powerless to stop the Achim."

Chapter 15

Drachen und Löwen

(Dragon and Lions)

Once more we see mention another "Cheva", and in von Hemrick's notes he ponders if these "Cheva" still exist in the deserts or other places in the world, just waiting to be discovered. He speculates if they could be used as some sort of spirit-beast weapon if they were "tamed" in some fashion.

This section, relates to the prophetic book of Daniel 14, and the novella book of Tobit dealing with the demon Asmodeus. We also see the appearance of another known biblical angel, Raphael.

Unlike previous sections where the forces of good interfere with the forces of evil's plans resulting in some prophetic future plan, this time there seems to be a lesson on how the leadership of the Satan works (which is as expected is not nice to say the least).

1 It came to pass that Akamu Nebuchadnezzar was succeeded by Akamu Astyages, and the Adriel Daniel was still the advisor.

2 Under Adriel Daniel's direction Akamu Nebuchadnezzar had destroyed all that Asmodeus had built by the Akamu living in the lands of the East.

3 No more would they worship the pesel we had them make, and even the kohen of the pesels were killed.

4 The Adriel Daniel even managed to kill the Cheva Tannin which we had the Akamu worship by feeding it as ordered by Hosek so as to keep its strength up since it was bound.

5 Enraged by these actions, Asmodeus inspired Akamu Astyages to kill Adriel Daniel by having him thrown into a pit with starving beasts.

6 We Achim gathered about to watch and wait for the neharbeyheem of the Adriel Daniel to be released by these beasts.

7 But instead a small group of Guardian Uri descended into the pit.

8 We Achim hid from their sight, and watched as they calmed the beasts so they would just lie there or simply walk about uninterested in the Adriel Daniel.

9 This continued for days until the sixth day when from the heavens came a Guardian Uri holding an Adriel by the hair of his head.

10 I immediately recognized the Guardian Uri as Aya, but I did not know this Adriel she had brought.

11 The Adriel said his name was the prophet Habakkuk and handed the Adriel Daniel a small cake, which he graciously took and ate.

12 At which point the Guardian Uri Aya again flew off with the Adriel Habakkuk by holding the hair of his head.

13 Upon the seventh day the Akamu Astyages came to mourn for the Adriel Daniel, but instead found him alive and well.

14 At which point Akamu Astyages rejoiced and released the Adriel Daniel proclaiming him to be a great prophet of the Adriel, and he also praised Adonai.

15 Asmodeus ordered the Achim there to retreat for a time to a place outside in the desert.

16 I was called by Hosek and reported to him all that had transpired.

17 With Hosek was the slender Achim known as Yahnah.

18 I had thought Yahnah had been captured by the Uri recently and imprisoned in the Shuchah of the Tehom.

19 I did not understand how he got out exactly, because I thought no Achim could get out of this Uri prison.

20 "Zuriel, my most trusted servant, please take this message to Asmodeu", Hosek said as he handed me a small stone. "I plan to reassign Asmodeus to a different task in the Akamu lands known as Media where he will be responsible for dealing with one particular Adriel living there. I would like both you and Yago to go with Asmodeus on this task, but you and Yago are not to get involved but simple watch from a distance. Do you understand these commands?"

21 Hosek asked as I nodded in response.

22 So it came to pass that I, and Yago, returned to Asmodeus, who was brooding in the desert over his defeats in the lands of the East, and I gave him the stone from Hosek.

23 Privately he read the stone, and then turned to the Achim present saying that he would no longer be their commander. Another will come shortly to replace him.

24 With that he turned to Yago and me and said, "It seems I am to go to the Akamu lands of Media to torture the Adriel Sarah. Hosek says you both are come with me, but not aide me. Did he say anything else to either of you?"

responding to his query I said nothing more than what was written on the stone.

25 "I see. Then let us proceed at once," Asmodeus sniped.

26 In the Akamu lands of Media, we came upon the house of the Adriel Sarah.

27 As was their custom she was to have a berith ownah, but as instructed Asmodeus would each time would proceed to frighten each Akamu chathan or Adriel chathan to the point that it would cause the release of their neharbeyheem.

28 This continued for some time, and one after another Asmodeus would cause the release of their neharbeyheems.

29 But then one night, as Yago and I watched, we noticed that the Adriel Sarah started some incense which quickly filled her chamber.

30 The smell was very terrible to us and we kept our distance, but Asmodeus was unaware and proceeded as before as the new Adriel chathan entered the Adriel Sarah's chamber.

31 Just then Asmodeus was overtaken by the smell of the incense and began to flee.

32 Both Yago and I followed him all the way to the desert lands of Matsor.

33 There he came to rest, and Yago and I hid behind a rock so as not to be seen.

34 Just then from the heavens descended a Tartan Uri known as Raphael.

35 He quickly grabbed Asmodeus and wrestled him to the ground.

36 Asmodeus fought back but the Tartan Uri Raphael's grip was too strong for him since he

was weakened by the pungent smell of the incense.

37 Then to my surprise I watched as the Tartan Uri Raphael pulled from his belt what looked like an asuk, and in an instant Asmodeus was no more.

38 Then the Tartan Uri Raphael again returned to the heavens, and both Yago and I were in so much fear; we hid for a time in the desert lands of Mastor before returning to Hosek.

39 Upon returning to Hosek, I reported all that had transpired.

40 "You have done well, Zuriel" he said. But I asked if he knew about the asuk the Uri have in their possession. "Yes I am aware of the asuk they have. It is used only by certain Tartan Uri to send Akim to Shuchah."

41 I dared to ask Hosek if he knew Asmodeus would be captured, and he said, "I was aware this would happen. It was all part of the deal for Yahnah's release. I had no more need for Asmodeus, and I needed Yahnah more so. So I struck a deal with the Uri to exchange the one for the other."

42 "But I saw Yahnah with you before the capture of Asmodeus," I exclaimed to Hosek, "couldn't you have just gone back on the deal? Asmodeus was invaluable to us when we gave tsaphad to the Akamu; he was the one who gave it to the Adriel after the campaign in the lands of Mastor."

43 Hosek calmly responded, "Oh Zuriel, why I do what I do is not for you to know just as much as you cannot see beyond the nothingness. Now leave me before I decide to turn you over the Uri as well."

44 I left Hosek to ponder all these events.

45 It was true I could not see beyond the nothingness of my own fate, nor could I see the outcomes of the actions of others unless they revealed it to me.

46 But the events of recent things concerned me. Was I to end up like Asmodeus; to end up in Shuchah?

47 I was not certain for I did not know what Shuchah was like, except it was in the Tehom.

48 And what was with Yahnah? I never did like him for he felt like slime to me, but seemed to be one that Hosek favored a lot with certain assignments involving both the Akamu and Adriel from the very beginning of things.

49 He was slender and sly, clever and devious. One who was very convincing, firm, and had a certain air of charisma about him. He so easily convinced both Akamu and Adriel to follow slavish ideas with little resistance.

50 He was responsible for teaching both Akamu and Adriels that their ishshah were rekush, and he was in charge of the campaign in the lands of Mastor against the Adriels; something that landed him in Shuchah as far as I was aware.

51 The more I pondered all these things, the more I felt the grip of the nothingness approaching me; the endless nothingness where we will all go.

die Zwei

(The Two)

This part appears to be related to the Zurvanist Zoroastrian dualistic myth of light and dark realms eternally locked in battle which is counted by the typical Jewish understandings of idolatry, represented here by the well-known assistant to Jeremiah, Baruch. The Gnostic heresy of Manichaeism owes its underpinnings to the Zurvanist Zoroastrian myth itself.

This translation is an evident expansion of Chapter 6 of Baruch, the Letter of Jeremiah, which was only known to be in Greek but may originally have been in Hebrew. The interesting thing about the Book of Baruch is that it is considered by many scholars to be "fictionally" set in Babylon and edited sometime in the last couple of centuries BCE. While I personally don't think this distracts from the content of the message, for some out there it throws into question its "spiritual authenticity."

With this particular translation there are also elements from Det. 34 mentioning the death of Moses, and Jude 9 which also mentions the death of Moses in reference to a text known as the "Assumption of Moses.".

I am uncertain what the writer is trying to do with this particular text, but it may be an attempt to water down certain concepts to ensure that it is preserved. Dualism has since Irenaeus and before being rejected by Christian and Jews alike. The belief in an eternal dualistic spiritual reality was very popular with the Gnostics. But for Irenaeus, and the other Christian scholars, the notion of two kinds of eternities would create the possibility of two eternal Godheads, one good and one evil. The only other option would be to have one supreme eternal Godhead controlling both good and evil eternities, but then said Godhead is no longer really a "loving" Godhead and more of neutral entity administering to the other eternal creatures living in the two eternal realms. Then the question becomes can you even have an eternal master Godhead controlling two forms of eternities or would this make yet a third eternity where the master Godhead resides? It is no wonder that these kinds of thoughts were simply rejected for the view of a single eternity controlled by a single Godhead.

1 Hosek called to me and said the following, "My most faithful rock, I am going to need you to go to the lands of the east once more to see what Elisheva is planning. I had an agreement with Adonai concerning the neharbeyheem of the Adriel Mashah since the end of the campaign in the lands of Matsor, and I believe Elisheva is going to fulfill their side of the bargain."

2 "But mighty Hosek, I thought it was impossible for them to gather back the entire scattered Adriels?" I responded.

3 Hosek continued, "It would seem we did not scatter them far enough. And now I will have to release to the Uri the neharbeyheem of the Adriel Moses to them unless we can stop the Uri. We almost got the Adriels to worship the Adriel Mashah like some of the Akamu do, but I was forbidden to reveal his grave to the Adriels. My only consolation was being able to hold on to the neharbeyheem of the Adriel Mashah unless the Uri could gather back the Adriels scattered among the Akamu. Now go quickly to the lands of the east and find the Adriel Baruch who has been sent to bring the message of their return."

4 And so I came upon a place in the lands of the east where the Adriel Baruch was standing in the midst of many Adriels and the Adriel Coniah, with them was also many Akamu come to listen to the words of the Adriel Baruch.

5 I could see scattered among them some Guardian Uri, and upon a roof top stood Elisheva watching over the entire assembly.

6 The Adriel Baruch spoke these words, "I, Baruch have traveled from the Yerushalem to bring to you the words of the prophet Ramam", and then he proceeded to unwind a scroll and continued, "For your transgressions, Adonai has spoken that you shall remain in the lands of the east for seven generations but then you shall return by His hand. While you live in the lands of the east you will see many gods who cannot speak as Adonai does, but have tongues of silver, gold and wood. Take heed of them and do not follow them. Do not participate in their festivals, their booths, or follow behind them in the streets as they are carried about the city for they have no feet. Their kohen will take their offerings and use it for their own uses, for the offerings will not go to these gods as they have tongues that have been smoothed and polished of silver, gold and wood which cannot speak as Adonai does. These false kohen will entice you with words of luxury and promises of zanah at no cost. These gods are as useless as a broken pot. Their kohen will light lamps to them, but still will not see the truth. Do not fear their tricks and words, for Adonai will set a guardian to be with you always. A guardian who shall bring you back as Adonai has said He would do", and upon finishing the Adriel Baruch rolled up the scroll again.

7 As Adriel Baruch spoke these words, several Akamu kohen came to see what the commotion was about for they had heard that Adriel Baruch was reading a scroll from the prophet Ramam.

8 Once Adriel Baruch was done, the chief Akamu kohen took a position before the crowd and with his fellow kohen standing by his side and he proclaimed the following, "The great maker god, Ki has twenty names and he is to be worshiped. We are to worship the good, the strong, the beneficent, the earth, and the neharbeyheem of the wild beasts, the neharbeyheem of holy chathan and ishshah, and the rauch that walk the lands of the earth."

9 The chief Akamu kohen continued, "In the beginning there was the great galgal of nothing; the invisible eternal nothing from which the great maker god Ki made all and begot his two sons, Arum and Shachar. The two sons are to rule the eternal lands of light and dark; Arum for light and Shachar for dark. The lands of light are pure rauch, and the lands of dark are pure earth. Shachar took a wife Kazab from which all the people of the earth came. The great maker god Ki has let his two sons determine the fate of all and cares not who wins, for he has moved on to other things. These are the truths of the world, the only truths to be known, and what Baruch speaks of is nothing more than tricks and lies."

10 Adriel Baruch stood once more before the crowd, and I could see that Elisheva had a very stern look upon his face as the Adriel Baruch pushed aside the chief Akamu kohen and other kohen to stand before the crowd.

11 The other Guardian Uri present among the crowd appeared to be ready as if to do battle, and then Adriel Baruch spoke these words, "The words of the prophet Ramam are for those who are true Adriel. If any Adriel would believe and follow the words of these false kohen then an eternal punishment will be upon

them as long as they follow them. For these words are not of Adonai, and speak of ways that are false. There is but one eternity and it is Adonai. Only Adonai is good, and all He made is good which includes all of the earth, beasts, and people. For we all know what is written in the beginning that upon finishing making all of creation Adonai saw it was good. While it is true for a time the Adriel who live here must be here, it is not true that they must follow false gods. They are to keep to their ways of their fathers before them, the ways Adonai has taught them. No command of any Akamu malak or false kohen can tell them to worship another god, no matter how forceful the command is" at which point Adriel Baruch turned quickly and took his seat again.

12 The Akamu kohen were flushed with anger at Adriel Baruch's words and just then Elisheva stretched out his right hand and the Guardian Uri present in the crowd began to touch the Adriel and Akamu present causing each to leave quietly.

13 Even the Akamu kohen, despite their initial anger, were touched by the Guardian Uri and simply left calmly instead.

14 Upon watching the dispersion of the Adriel and Akamu, I also took my leave of this place.

15 But I had not found what Elisheva was planning.

16 Hosek was correct in that Adonai was going to make good on the deal that was made, but how this was to happen I had not discovered as of yet.

17 I could not return to Hosek until I had this information for I did not wish to end up like Asmodeus.

18 I sat outside the Akamu city in the desert as the vision of the nothingness gripped me once more.

Chapter 17

Greifen nach Gleichheit

(Grasping at Equality)

von Hemrick's notes calls this section, "Grasping at Equality". I think he was referring to the New Testament passage from Paul's Letter to the Philippians 2:6 where it mentions Jesus' divine equality with God as something Jesus did not grasp at; which is an odd reflection because most of this translation seems to be related to passages from the book of Ezekiel. Although the Book of Ezekiel is considered one of the most relevant Old Testament texts dealing with the prophesied Messiah; the one who would free the Jewish people in bondage.

This particular translation seems to take place when the prophet Ezekiel is in captivity. It is my understanding that he is the only prophet of God in the Old Testament to be outside of the Holy Land. It is also said of him that he was a temple Priest at the time of the conquest of Judah. With this particular translation, we also see the mechanism of how God communicated to Ezekiel (i.e. Through an Angel of the Lord). This concept is very common for it is understood that "direct communication" with God is just not difficult, but can be really harmful to humans in our current state of being. So traditionally such messages were always thought to be brought through some lesser spiritual entity who could tolerate getting the message from God and then relaying it to humans. Sometimes this is done by the entity revealing itself as an angel, other times a dream, other times just some voice from the sky. Even so usually the message would provoke some form of awe and wonder primarily because of its source (i.e. God), although on occasion the human getting the message has been known to ask questions about it or not understand what was exactly said at first.

With this particular translation, that while Ezekiel is relaying what is told to him to his own people he is actually relaying the message to Zuriel who happens to be listening at the time. It is understood among certain academic circles that despite the fact that angels are spiritual creatures with incredible knowledge and foresight; they still are unable to know everything like God (despite what the Satan would have us believe otherwise). Being created beings like us, God chooses how to reveal things to them in His own way and own time, but the fallen angels are understood to be cut off from this knowledge in a permanent way due to their decision not to follow God. Even so, this doesn't mean God doesn't stop talking to the fallen angels. Clearly, with this passage He is talking to Zuriel so Zuriel can relay the message to Hosek (i.e. The Satan). The problem is due to their permanent fallen state that the message is just factual to them or a series of words without a spiritual understanding to them. Their fallen state of being does not allow them to comprehend the greater meaning of the words spoken and never will, which of course God would know. So why would God do such a thing? Beats me, but God does many a thing we do not understand, nor are we meant to necessarily understand at times and such is His ways. Hence the claim by the Jewish people in book of Ezekiel four times that God's justice was not equal or is basically unfair.

1 For a time I waited in the desert outside the Akamu city, and word came to me that there was one of the Adriel Kohen who was speaking in the name of Adonai.

2 So with haste I went to where he was to listen to his words.

3 Gathered around were many Adriel who had come to listen to the Adriel Kohen's words.

4 Present were also the Guardian Uri, but I did not see Elisheva.

5 Even so I hid nearby to listen to this Adriel Kohen's words, and this is what he said, "I will deliver them from every place where they were scattered in the day of dark clouds. I will send a Shepherd to be their guide. The Shepherd will sort the goats from the sheep. I, Adonai have promised to do these things; they

shall happen. Each will be judged, and if those who do not follow the ways of Adonai repent then they will be judged worthy. Those to be found unworthy will find themselves in an eternal saraph shakah like the children of Gay Hinnom."

6 At which point those Adriel present became indignant to what was being said and complained bitterly that Adonai's ways were not takan and had no sense of justice. Again the Adriel Kohen spoke the same with greater force in his words that each would be judged accordingly by the one coming to shepherd them from this imprisonment.

7 After this the crowd dispersed, and I retired again to the desert outside thc Akamu city.

8 During the night I saw a light of what appeared to be a Uri coming down to the Akamu city.

9 With great haste I went to where the light was going only to find it entering the chamber of Adriel Kohen who spoke earlier that day.

10 As I hid in the shadows, the light spoke to the sleeping Adriel Kohen and said the following, "I am the Tsir Uri Geber El, and once more come to you Adriel Ezekiel with a message from Adonai. Speak these words to your fellow Adriel in the morning- When I brought the Adriel from the lands of Mastor, they rejected me. I taught them my ways, and they rejected me. I took pity on them and ended their days in the wilderness, and yet they still rejected me. Therefore, I let them become gaal before me as every first born from the womb was saraph before me. And yet they would not turn. So I, Adonai will attack the lands of Magog and Gog. I will draw my sword

against them. With a great fire I will attack these lands, and I will not spare any of the kashal for they have chosen their path. There is no way back for them. I will rid the lands of every wild beast. My ways are just and takan and always have been since the beginning before your fathers where born; for I will blow my trumpet before my Shepherd. I am the eternal one, and I will be sending my Shepherd to guide my people back to me for this I have promised."

11 The Uri left as he came, and so did I.

12 I returned to Hosek to report all that I had heard and seen.

13 "Zuriel, my faithful rock, you have done well' Hosek said and continued, 'So it would seem Adonai will fight us after all, and what of this Shepherd the Adriel speak of? Who do you think he is?"

14 I answered, "Mighty Hosek, it can only be one person which the Uri speak of; that of Adoani's Omer."

15 "Yes I believe you are correct. I know we can stop Adoani's Omer so that I do not need to release the neharbeyheem of the Adriel Mashah. The one known as Gur will be our great weapon against the takan ways of Adonai. For after Hayyah, during the 26th day of Iyyar, the one whose number is 760 will speak against the takan ways of Adonai for us just as taught by Gur. It is because of Gur they will continue to reject the ways of Adonai and they will continue to take every first born from the womb and saraph them before him, and it will be seen as takan to them; all things will be seen takan to them no matter what prophet is sent by Adonai. Let us go now and prepare for things to come."

16 And so I left with Hosek to prepare for the pending war.

Chapter 18

Engel des Dieners

(Angels of the Servant)

The book of Obadiah is one of the shortest books in the Old Testament concerning the prophets, and one whose authorship debatable. The true authorship is unknown, but is attributed to Obadiah, a servant of Yah. There are many names in the Old Testament, which are linked to being a servant of Yah, such as Meshullam, Zechariah, Nathan, and Shimi to name a few. All such names are also linked to being a member of Isr. It is of unknown origin and may be referring to a country or land, like Assyria. This would make some sense of the Book of Obadiah because the actual text of Obadiah refers to Edomites who sided with the Assyrians when they destroyed the temple in Jerusalem in 587 BCE. The Edomites were a group of Jewish descendants, so this was seen as a real betrayal at the time.

With this particular translation we see a sort of spiritual conversation between the Fallen Angel, Zuriel and what appear to be four Cherubim. It is a little hard to follow because of the way it was written, but I think this was done on purpose to show how each Cherubim talked in turns versus one of them just speaking. I guess it is to show how they are sort of connected spiritually. Of particular note, this passage seems to get into the nature and fate of the Fallen Angels overall, while also still dealing with the issue of the soul of Moses.

1 I was called by Hosek and came to him, and as I did he was talking to someone I could not see.

2 As soon as I arrived, Hosek turned to me, and the other had left.

3 Hosek then spoke these words, "My faithful rock, I need you to go to the Akamu lands to the east. There outside one of their cities will be an Adriel by the name of Obadyahu. He will be in a cave, and you should find him asleep during the middle of the day. What I am about to say to you next you must remember, for what you will see and hear upon finding the Adriel Obadyahu you may not understand but it is important that your tell me all you see and hear. For the message you are about to receive will aide our cause and help me keep the neharbeyheem of the Adriel Mashah."

4 So at once I left for the Akamu lands to the east and as Hosek said I found sleeping in a cave during the middle of the day the one known Adriel Obadyahu.

5 As I approached the cave, a strong wind and clouds began to blow up from the east, and yet Adriel Obadyahu remained asleep in the cave.

6 From the clouds came out four lesser zoons, they were like the eternal zoons atop the Tower but smaller in nature. They darted about like gnats as they approached.

7 "What do you want? Are you here for the Adriel?" I asked the darting lesser zoons.

8 This is what they said as one in turn came to my face and said but a part of the words,

9 'Kashal, Son of Adonai, our words'

10 'Are not for the Adriel'

11 'But are from Adonai to you'

12 'Kashal, Son of Adonai'

13 'Then speak so that I may know these words!' I demanded. And again as before each

one in turn came to my face and spoke the following,

14 'Listen well then'

15 'For we will only speak them once'

16 'But you will not understand'

17 'For you have made your bachar'

18 "Then what use is it for you to talk to me, if I will not understand what you are about to say?!" I retorted back at the darting gnats, and again each one in turn came to my face and spoke the following,

19 'Kashal, Son of Adonai'

20 'You have already heard'

21 'The words of Adonai'

22 'And wisely determined the name of the Shepherd'

23 "It was not hard to determine the name of the Shepherd," I boasted, and again each one in turn came to my face and spoke the following,

24 'Yes this is true'

25 'But you did not'

26 'Understand what was'

27 'Said'

28 "Stop speaking in riddles you gnats, and tell me your message!" I demanded. Once more each in turn came to my face and spoke the following,

29 'Listen then'

30 'Kashal, Son of Adonai'

31 'For what we will say'

32 'We will say but once'

33 Then the lesser zoons paused for a moment,
as they darted about the air, and then
continued to speak as before,

34 'Those Adriel'

35 'Who are Akan'

36 'Descendants of'

37 'Asah, son of Isaac'

38 'Those who live'

39 'In the land'

40 'Of Adom'

41 'Will no longer be in favor'

42 'Adonai will'

43 'Cut them off'

44 'From all that is'

45 'Promised to them'

46 'For it is said'

47 'Jacob and Joseph'

48 'Will be a fire'

49 'Against Asah'

50 'To set ablaze'

51 'And devour it'

52 'None will survive'

53 'Of the house of Asah'

54 'In the day of calamity'

55 'One is not to gloat'

56 'One is not to'

57 'Lay hands on possessions'

58 'Nations who drink'

59 'Wrongly on the Holy Mountain'

60 'Will become as'

61 'They had not been'

62 'Adom was like'

63 'Foreigners'

64 'Casting lots for'

65 'The city of Yerushalem'

66 'What Adom has'

67 'Done'

68 'Adom will be'

69 'Done away with forever'

70 'Adom used to'

71 'Be like the eagle'

72 'Among the stars'

73 'But no more'

74 'For Zoon have been'

75 'Placed'

76 'To the East'
77 'Before all eternity'

78 'To guard'
79 'The way back'
80 'So none'
81 'Will come'

82 'Now Adom'
83 'Will be placed'
84 'In the Shuchah'
85 'For a time'

86 'But Adom'
87 'Will see'
88 'What lies East'
89 'Of eternity'

90 'For Adom'
91 'And all who follow'
92 'Like those in'
93 'Adom'

94 'They will all'
95 'End up'
96 'Being thrown'
97 'In the Saraph Mabbau'

98 'There is no escape'

99 'For them'

100 'There is no bribe'

101 'To free them'

102 'The Saraph Mabbau'

103 'Will sting more'

104 'Then did the bites'

105 'Of the Seraphim to the Adriel in desert'

106 'For a time those'

107 'In the Saraph Mabbau'

108 'Will be watched'

109 By the Uri and Adonai's Omer'

110 'But for many'

111 'Those who follow Adom'

112 'They will see'

113 'The Saraph Mabbau'

114 'A painful'

115 'Eternal'

116 'Fiery'

117 'Nothing'

118 'Except'

119 'There will be one'

120 'One who will be'

121 'With himself'

122 'For this one'

123 'He will be'

124 'Forever'

125 'Trapped'

126 'Never to'

127 'Be released'

128 'But promised'

129 'Eternity of Biqqoreth'

130 'Adonai will'

131 'Make good'

132 'One His promise'

133 'And the one held will be freed'

134 Then as they finished speaking, all four of the lesser zoon darted back up into the clouds and out of sight.

135 By now the sun was lower in the sky and the Adriel Obadyahu awoke from his sleep.

136 He got up, took from a satchel a scroll, a small bottle, and quill. He then began to write down some words.

137 From behind a rock I tried to read what he was writing, but it made no sense to me.

138 It spoke of Adom, and parts of what was said by the four lesser zoons as if he had a dream about it.

139 It was true what the lesser Zoons said that most of what was said to me I could not understand the meaning.

140 And yet I had to say something to Hosek upon my return.

141 So I left the Adriel Obadyahu and stayed in the desert for a time to ponder the meaning of the words of the lesser zoons.

142 But the more I thought of what was said the more I could only see the vision of the nothing that was before me.

143 They did speak of the nothing, an eternal nothing.

144 It was true this vision of the nothing was a fiery pain to me, like all the Achim.

145 All but one Achim, who was Hosek, this one thought gave me the strength to return to Hosek and tell him what I had learned from the four lesser zoons.

146 And this is what Hosek said to me, "Zuriel, my rock, you have done well once more. For now, we know more than we did before and while I am displeased by these words from Adonai we will need to make plans for retribution. Adonai will make good on his promise, and it seems l will have to release the neharbeyheem of the Adriel Mashah to the Uri. But listen to me, during Hege I will induce the brothers of Mastor to rachats the sepher sipharah and write the false words. Then during Hemes I will induce the twin sons of Apollo to spend their gold and silver to build a smoothed tongued pesel so as to cause the kohen of the Adriel to spend great sums from their treasuries to remove it. But this will be in vain for the smoothed tongued pesel will gather acolytes who will proclaim the false words from the brothers of Mastor to all who will hear as hidden truth from the beginning of things. Then and only then will my debt be paid to me for the loss of the neharbeyheem of the Adriel Mashah."

die klagende Sohn

(The Lamenting Son)

*This is a fascinating section in that it is combining two elements of both
the Old Testament and New Testament. In this story the element similar
to that of the Prodigal Son, who asks for his inheritance only to squander
it and then return to his father asking forgiveness, but instead with this
chapter we see elements of the Books of Lamentations chapter 3 which is
about the voice of the suffering individual. What is more fascinating is
the bit of revelation concerning human lamentation by the writer Zuriel;
where Zuriel ponders the very mystery of why humans are able to obtain
forgiveness and start again.*

1 It came to be that I was assigned to work under Beelzebul in the lands to the east.

2 Beelzebul was responsible for the flies of the campaign in Mastor, but now was given greater duties as part of a longer term plan in dealing with the upcoming return of the neharbeyheem of the Adriel Mashah.

3 He gave me the simple task of entering a young Adriel who was the son of an Adriel merchant.

4 The Adriel merchant had a large family, and although in exile managed to become well respected by both his fellow Adriels and the Akamus as a fair and just merchant.

5 This respect allowed him to do very well in the lands to the east.

6 So at night I entered the chambers of the young Adriel and inspired him through dreams that his other brothers and sisters would leave him with nothing when it came time for the Achim to take his neharbeyheem.

7 Night after night I would enter his chamber; and night after night I would feed him dreams of how he was left nothing from his father's estate.

8 In time the young Adriel became convinced that he would not get anything from his father's wealth and became angry at his other brothers and sisters for squandering their father's wealth on food and parties for their friends.

9 Then I crept in one night into his chambers and whispered into his ear, "Ask for your share of your father's estate now before your brothers and sisters spend it all, leaving you nothing."

10 The next morning while the family was gathered for the morning meal, the young Adriel stood up and demanded his share of his father's estate now.

11 All were in horror at such an act except his father.

12 His father stood up and asked the young Adriel, "Are you sure this is your wish?"

13 "It is" the young Adriel replied.

14 "Then it shall be as you have asked."

15 So the father later that day tallied his estate and divided out what would be the young Adriel's share.

16 The young Adriel then left his father's house to go make a name for him.

17 The young Adriel gathered his friends and he hosted celebrations and feasts.

18 He bought fine clothes for himself and rings for his fingers.

19 Young ishshah who sought nothing but zanah sat at his feet.

20 And each night I would whisper to him what more could be done with his inheritance.

21 Soon his spirit's mind was filled with what I had said to him, and his spirit's heart had dimmed just enough for me to slip into him one night.

22 No more would I whisper things to the young Adriel at night, now I would walk with him in the day and enjoy all that he does.

23 His spirit's mind was mine to shape like that of a potter, and his spirit's heart would in time become stone.

24 And so day after day and night after night, for forty long days I walked with young Adriel and he put up no resistance to my dwelling with him.

25 I became intoxicated with his youth and lack of matsar in his being.

26 Now I understood what Yago had meant by the anah of the Adriel and Akamu.

27 Such power and such strength all from one Adriel who's neharbeyheem could be taken from him. This was something I did not want to end.

28 But one morning, outside the Akamu city it would come to an end.

29 For that morning the young Adriel awoke to find himself upon a camel dung heap being poked with stick by the Camel Master.

30 His purse was empty, his clothes were stained, his shoes were gone, and he smelled.

31 Then the young Adriel did an odd thing, something I could not stop. He got up from the dung heap, fell upon the ground and began to weep.

32 The more he wept, the more his spirit's heart awoke. The harder it was for me to stay with him.

33 He began to say to with his arms stretched out to the heavens, "I truly deserve this dung heap for my home. I have forsaken all that my father has taught me, all that our people are to believe. I have nothing to show for all that I have done and my deeds if tallied amount to nothing in the book. I have squandered all that was given to me and have sinned against my father, my people, and Adonai. I was a fool to reject all that I was taught. Now even this Camel Master will not take me. I have spent all my life in an instant and will Adonai restore it? Will my father take me back? I am the shame of our family and people. I deserve to live in the desert with the goats that are sent there. Over and over I am downcast, but this I will call to mind and therefore I will hope. Adonai's mercy is not spent nor exhausted, for it is renewed each morning. It is said it is good to be young and to bear the yoke. To put one's mouth in the dust for there may yet be hope. My life is now in the pit and I have said 'I am lost!', but I hope in you Adonai. Hear my plea and do not let your ear be deaf to my cry of help."

34 At this point the young Adriel fell to the ground once more and began to bitterly weep, and his spirit's heart came alive and shown with a bright light.

35 So bright was its light I could not stay with him and found myself beside him.

36 This is when I caught sight of the Guardian Uri Aya standing at the other side of the camel pen, her arms were crossed at first but then she began to reach for the sword at her side.

37 This is when I left for the deserts outside the Akamu city, and the Guardian Uri Aya did not follow.

38 For over 120 days I waited in the deserts outside the Akamu city before I would return with seven of my brothers as per Beelzebul's instructions.

39 There I pondered the meaning of the young Adriel's cry to heaven; His plea to Adonai for help which made no sense to me.

40 For when I walked with him I could still see before me the nothingness that I had always seen.

41 Every choice I made him do would lead to the nothingness; an unalterable course for which there is no return.

42 And yet somehow these Adriel and even the Akamu are able to alter their course. They are able to turn back on themselves and start again anew as if nothing had occurred.

43 What is it that allows them to do this? Could it be the brightness of their spirit's heart?

44 I have watched many an Adriel and Akamu both cry and weep as I took the neharbeyheem

of some friend, a father or mother, a brother or sister.

45 All do the same crying out to the heavens for help. But help never comes, except this one time help came.

46 The Guardian Uri Aya, she came to this young Adriel's side.

47 Was it she who brightened his heart? It must have been for no Adriel or Akamu have such power inside them as far as I was concerned.

48 For it is more common that if their spirit's heart be restless against us as we walk with them it will cause them act oddly before their fellow Adriel and Akamu; thinking they are mad or insane and it becomes difficult for an Achim to control.

49 Yes, the Guardian Uri Aya must have done something to force me out. She must have awakened his spirit's heart somehow.

50 This is the only truth to the problem before me.

26th day of Iyyar - This is day in the Jewish calendar of the Month of Iyyar.

Achim - This word means "constructed by God". It appears that the writer is suggesting that at first the angels were collectively all the same, but later became something different.

Achzib- this is the village where Judah's wife, Shua had her third son (Genesis 38:5).

Adom - This word means "to be red" and is referring to the lands of Edom where those who are descendants of Esau were settled.

Adonai - This word means "Lord". Okay, this one is sort of obvious who the writer is talking about. No decoder ring needed here.

Adonai's bayith and hekal- these words mean God's House and Palace/Temple. I think this is referring to Solomon's Temple or possibly the future temple to be built by the Messiah.

Adonai's neshama-nur- these words basically mean God's breathe fire. I think this is in reference to the Holy Spirit and how the Holy Spirit overshadowed Mary during the conception of Jesus.

Adonai's Omer- this set of words means God's word or promise. I do believe this is referring directly to the Messiah (i.e. Christ).

Adriel Ahaziah - He was the King of Judah about 841 BCE succeeds Jehoram of Judah. He is killed in Megiddo and is supposed to be buried in the City of David (i.e. Jerusalem).

Adriel Athaliah - She was the Queen of Judah from about 842 to 836 BCE and mother of King Ahaziah.

Adriel Baruch - This is a clear reference to Baruch, the secretary of the prophet Jeremiah.

Adriel chathan - This word means the same as Akamu chathan, except is referring to the Adriel instead.

Adriel Coniah - This is one of three names given to the Judean king deposed and exiled in Babylon. The others are Jeconiah and Jehoiachin. He was king of Judah from 598 to 597 BCE.

Adriel Daniel and Companions- This is clearly a reference to the prophet Daniel and his three companions; Shadrach, Meshach, and Abednego.

Adriel Ezekiel - This is the prophet Ezekiel.

Adriel Habakkuk - This of course is the prophet Habakkuk. He is mentioned in Daniel 14 basically as described in this text and in the Bible where he was making a cake for himself when an angel plucked him from Judea to feed Daniel. Habakkuk also has his own prophetic book in the Bible as well.

Adriel ishshah - This word is similar to Akamu ishshah usage except it is referring to the women of the followers of God instead.

Adriel Job- This is a clear and direct reference to the Book of Job and specifically Job himself.

Adriel Mashah - The word "mashah" means to draw out or drew out. Usually this word is thought to be a precursor word for Mosheh, or Moses. Based on the translation of the text, I do believe the person being talked of here is Moses, or more specifically in the text the state of his soul (which is a subject of considerable debate in some circles).

Adriel Obadyahu - This is a reference to the author of the Book of Obadiah. Obadyahu is an older Hebrew name meaning servant of Yah (Lord).

Adriel Sarah - This is a direct reference to the Sarah mentioned in the book of Tobit who marries Tobiah, son of Tobit. She is the one plagued by the demon Asmodeus, who kills each suitor before the marriage is consummated, and with the help of Tobiah and the Angel Raphael rids her of this demon.

Adriel- This means "follower of God", and is a clear reference to the Jewish people and all the humans who follow the one true God.

Akamu - This is a clear reference to humanity as the word means formed by God from the earth.

Akamu Astyages - A king of the Median Empire during 585-550 BCE, before Cyrus the Great.

Akamu chathan- these two words mean 'formed by God bridegroom'. I think is showing the relationship of man to woman in that the male was to be the bridegroom to woman. Obviously, though it is being used in a sense to designate maleness of the human race.

Akamu ibriy - this combination of words means "formed by God woman of Eber". Eber is also known as the lands of the Hebrews in some transliterations. Clearly the idea here is by the addition of the higher creator angels' spirit into the original human females that an even better human is made. This concept really seems to me to be an early Docetae-like idea of spiritual enlightenment.

Akamu ishshah - this combination of words means "formed by God female". Clearly the combination is to show a distinction between the spiritual world and material world.

Akamu Nebuchadnezzar- This is the King of the pre-Babylonian kingdom after the fall of the Assyrian Empire. He ruled from 605 to 562 BCE and is also known as Nebuchadnezzar II.

Akan - This is a word used to denote a descendant of Esau.

Akim - This word means "originating from God". Clearly the writer of the text is making some sort of distinction between angels and some higher order of beings that are closer to God.

Anah - this word means to defile.

Arum - This word means crafty or shrewd, and I think it is referring to the Zoroastrian god Ahura Mazda who lives in the realm of light and is the lord of wisdom.

Asah, Son of Isaac - Asah means to press or squeeze which is the root word for Esau. So this combination is referred to Esau, the son of Isaac.

Asmodeus - This is a demon and main antagonist mentioned in the book of Tobit, although interestingly, he appears in this text as the cause of the Assyrian attack upon and basic end of the Davidic Kingdoms.

Asuk- this means pot. It is clearly some sort of container which directly connects to the Abyss or Tehom. At this point in the book (assuming I am getting the order correct) this sort of makes sense from the perspective that Sheol was where all the souls (good or bad) went upon their death.

Aya- This word means bird or to fly swiftly. This word, in slightly different forms, is actually found in many languages from Turkish to Japanese to Cherokee. And in old German means sword. Although here it seems to be referring to a particular Angle of God, which is a "Guardian Angel", but I think the author of the text is not using this term in the modern understanding. It seems to me that the term "Guardian Angel" or "Guardian Uri" is referring more to a kind of rank or job. Sort of like a private in an army.

Bachar- this word means to choose. I think the writer here is making a reference to the first part where the Achim was separated into the Achim and Uri through a choice given by Adonai. It would appear this time the choice was given instead by Hosek through the object that Zuriel saw. This is a clear reference to the fall of man in Genesis, although not as sexual as some traditions have suggested, by the use of Eve and the snake (I know you would approve more so of this version Alyssa, as well as many other women on the planet).

Beelzebul - Beelzebul is known as the "Prince of Demons" and the meaning of the name is speculated to mean the 'lord of the house'. This demon is also known as the 'Lord of Flies'; flies usually meaning lesser demons, but in this case it seems to refer to plague that occurred in Exodus. Although with these writings, it seems that Beelzebul is now in charge of human possession. During Jesus' time and several years before it was a common Jewish practice of casting out demons from people. This practice is even mentioned in the writings of Josephus. Some scripture scholars have speculated that the dialogue that appears in the New Testament concerning Jesus' casting out of demons is actually an attempt to rebuke Jesus' authority to do so by the Temple hierarchy by discrediting the source of His power as it were.

Berith ownah- these two words basically mean 'covenant marriage'. Interestingly the word on does not appear, but once in the Hebrew texts and not at all in the Greek texts. Clearly, though a distinction in marriage contracts is being drawn here with the use of this word because covenants generally are unbreakable in nature and the contrasting use against tsaphad is to show how marriages could be broken in reference to the curse placed upon the woman in Genesis.

It is interesting how the writer is also hinting that this kind of marriage could lead to greater spiritual enlightenment vs. a standard contractual kind of marriage.

Beriths- this word means covenant, and I think this is in reference to the seven seals mentioned in the Book of Revelations especially since the four are named by colors corresponding to the colors of the four horsemen. It is interesting that this word is used for the seals because it seems to me that the text is trying to allude that the seals was for a certain time in the bible. Basically, that early time of the covenants the Lord God would make in Genesis.

Bethulah - this means virgin, and I am thinking here this is in reference to the Virgin Mary or the woman spoken of in the Book of Revelations. It appears to be alluding to the idea that "a virgin" will appear before all of mankind proclaiming the end of times.

Biqqoreth - This word means punishment.

Chadash- this means new. I think this is in reference to the part of the Book of Revelations where the new kingdom is established.

Chagowr - means belt or apron.

Chalal - this is an obvious negative sexual reference because it means prostitute. I think this is a direct reference to the curse laid upon the woman in Genesis (i.e. Eve). I think what is meant by this word use is more of how the man will see the woman or the relations between the two sexes will not in state as originally intended. Which is a mystery as to why have such a curse in the first place, I wonder if this text will get more into this issue which has plagued some scholars.

Chalaq- this word means to divide or split. A clear resultant of a basic contract theory to marriage is that it should be able to be divided up or split in some fashion should it be required (like any basic contract).

Cheva Lel - Cheva means beasts, and Lel is an earlier word for the demon Lilith. It is interesting how this text has tied the original story found in Genesis dealing with the Nephilim in Genesis 6:1-4 to this point in time as a greater explanation for certain kinds of demonic like beasts. Clearly, in the writer Zuriel is using the demoness Lilith to represent some form of a great beast like evil unleashed by the Satan.

Cheva Tannin - Cheva means beast, and tannin means a monster, serpent or dragon. This is a direct reference to the last chapter in Daniel where Daniel kills a "dragon".

Cheva-paal - this combination of words basically means "beast maker". I have no idea what it is in reference to exactly, but clearly humanity will be given the ability to make some sort of creatures.

Children of Gay Hinnom - This is a direct reference to the Valley of the Son of Hinnom where there was a practice of immolation of children took place, and later it would be known as Gehenna.

Chokmah - This word means wisdom, and in Hebrew it is the feminine. You see this word used in Proverbs and few other places referring to God's wisdom and the Truth of His ways. In this particular case it appears being used in the sense mentioned in Proverbs 8 where Wisdom is seen as a spirit or creature of God.

Dark Stars Loas- This phrase comes to translating "Bent Pole Peoples". I am not certain what this is in reference to exactly, but I suspect since stauros has usually come to refer to a cross that this might be a reference to those following a bent cross. I wonder if this text may have been known to the Nazis prior to the war or it could be the translation matrix itself is the problem to show their "importance" in history.

Echad-neged-azar - this combination of words means "one-in opposite to-helper" which I think is referring back to Genesis where Eve is created as Adam's helper and that Eve is both from Adam (as taken from his side) and is his opposite. Clearly the text is trying to allude to an original purpose or plan which has not gone as originally intended.

Edah of Omer - Edah means congregation and I think this is referring to what is used in Greek for Church (ekklesia), and in this context it would mean the Church of Promise or Christ's Church.

Elisheva - This word means "God is my wrath". I am not certain who this angel is exactly, but clearly like Hosek he is a leader angel of some kind.

Ervah- this word originates from arah which is to be naked or bare. But with this word, it means a shameful version of nakedness. This is a direct link the Noah story in Genesis where Noah exposes himself after drinking too much and then curses Ham's children.

Gaal - The word gaal has a few possible meanings. It can mean to redeem, but also to abhor or loath. It could also refer to a Canaanite. Although based on the translation I think it is referring to the verb "to defile".

Great Galgal - The word galgal means wheel, whirl or whirlwind and it is a clear reference to the Zoroastrian creation story concerning the great wheel of nothing from which all mater was made.

Great maschith - this means a great destruction.

Gur - This word means "sojourning, or dwelling" and is the place in Palestine, where King Ahaziah was wounded by those who opposed his reign. It is from this place that King Ahaziah would then leave only to die in Megiddo (hence sojourning I guess).

Halak-maveth-neharbeyheem - this combination of words includes an early word (neharbeyheem) which is oddly smashed together word roughly equivalent to soul (see earlier postings that contain the listing of transliterations). The other parts mean to go or walk (halak) and death (maveth) and taken all together would mean some sort of walking dead soul or basically a zombie soul (?).

Hosek - This word means "darkness". I am suspecting this person is the devil or the Satan. It is hard to tell because of the 4th Century the Satan was much more clearly defined as in opposition to God, and this character so far doesn't seem so but then again I am not finished with the text.

Karath- this word means to cut off or cut down and again another clear reference to the ability of basic contractual school of thought on marriage where the parties in question are cut off from each other when the contract terms cease to be enforced.

Kashal - This word means to stumble, or stagger.

Kashal, Son of Adonai - Kashal of course means to stumble or stagger, and in this case with the use Son of Adonai (Son of God), I think this is referring to the state of the angel himself (i.e. That of being fallen).

Kazab - This word means 'to lie', and I think it is referring to the Zoroastrian goddess Darj which is the wife to Aharman, and like Aharman is also evil and lives in the pit of the earth (i.e. Hell).

Ki - This word means 'because', but I think in the text, it is referring to the Zoroastrian creator god, and god of time and space, Zarvan. Zarvan is responsible for creating everything, including his two sons who control the eternal realms of light and dark all out of the stuff of nothing.

Kli - This means "vessel".

Kohen- this word means priest.

Lesser Zoons - Zoon of course means living creature, and I think this is referring to lower form of the four living creatures mentioned in Revelations that surround the throne of God. This would still technically make them a form of Cherubim.

Magog and Gog - These two names appear in the bible few times both in the Old Testament and New Testament. Sometimes Gog is a person, and sometimes like in this translation it appears as a place. Scholars have debated for some time exactly who these people are or where they are located, but according to the bible a war will be waged against them.

Malak- this word means to become a king or king.

Maphteach - this word means key. One can tell with the passage that the "Tower" where God resides contains "secret knowledge" known only to those angels that follow God. The key here I think is to represent the means to which one will obtain said knowledge. This passage could represent to a novice that if one has a certain pre-knowledge (i.e. The key) that one could get past any difficulties to obtain the true meanings and understandings. But I am just speculating here on a possible Gnostic meaning of things.

Mashach- this word means to anoint or smear. From this word comes Messiah.

Matsar - this word means control.

Matsor - This means Egypt, and appears to be referring to the part of Exodus where the first born were slain.

Maveth - This word means death. It makes some sense that the author Zuriel would not know of this idea being that of a spiritual dimension. All angels, fallen or not, are traditionally seen as pure spirit not bound by the concept of material death. Clearly by using this word the writer or writers (I still wonder if there were multiple authors since this text were found in the ruins of the monastery) are trying to show the major distinction between the material world and the spiritual world.

Media - This is the city where, according to the book of Tobit, Tobit left a sum of money on deposit. It is also the home of Sarah.

Mishchah - This means anointed or consecrated portion, and its use of the text appears to be referring to a dedicated follower of God, such as religious monks' maybe (?), or it could be something simpler since certain the Rites of Initiation are sometimes referred to as a process in which one becomes "consecrated" to God.

Navakalesen- Okay, this word is a bit harder to figure out. It appears to me that it is a combination of three words- Neva (meaning home), Kalil (meaning entire or whole), and chesen (meaning royal power). Taken all together, I think it means "keeps a home of the royal power". According to von Hemrick's notes he believes this is in reference to the name Emmerich or what we would know as Americus. Clearly this is some sort of foreshadowing of future events which von Hemrick believed would involve America in some fashion.

Neharbeyheem- This word appears to be a combination of three words mashed together- neharah, beyn, and eloheem. Or another words, "Light from God". Basically, this word is referring to our soul. I think the introduction of this word combination is referring to the part of Genesis where God mentions that His spirit is in humanity for a short time. This is especially true when you consider this text is saying that more zehman (or time) was needed for the addition of the Akim's spirit (or builder spirits).

Onyia - This means "ship".

Or-kuttoneth - means tunic.

Otto von Hemrick - Nazi Archaeologist who finds the text in Syria. Was a member of the Ahnenerbe.

Panim of Adonai - this means "Face of God". I think what this is referring to is a kind of meeting mentioned in the opening of the Book of Job where the Angels gathered before God. One could think of it as a gathering of a royal court.

Pesel - this word means image or idol.

Prophet Ramam - The word 'ramam' means to exalt, and I think this is the prophet Jeremiah (Jeremiah means may God exalt) because in the final chapter of the Book of Baruch it is titled 'the Letter from Jeremiah' and the whole of the translated text seems to deal with a scroll of this prophet.

Qetsaph- this word means wrath, and this is a clear reference to the Bowls in the Book of Revelations which are God's wrath poured out against humanity.

Rachats - This word means to bath or wash off.

Rauch- this word means wind, but in this case I think it is referring to a spiritual state. This is especially true because its use in reference to the Christ is consistent with the standard Gnostic view of the Christ being trapped here in this world wanting to return to God. It is also used to refer to the nature of the angels themselves later.

Rekush - This word means possessions, property or goods. Its use of this text is clear to denote women (and no doubt children) were nothing more than chattel to men. It could also be used to show even other humans in general were property (i.e. Slaves).

Sahed - This word means advocate and in Hebrew it is the masculine. I believe this word is referring technically to the Holy Spirit (i.e. The advocate mentioned by Jesus in John 16:7). Two of the known gifts of the Holy Spirit are wisdom and counsel. It would appear with this text that the creature Chokmah representing wisdom is working for and/or with the Holy Spirit in addition to the Messiah.

Saraph - This word means to have burned.

Saraph Mabbau - Saraph of course means to have burned, and mabbau means spring. I think this is referring to the fiery pool mentioned in Revelations where Satan and the damned are thrown into for all eternity.

Saraph Shakah - These two words mean "burned" and "to lay down", and I think this is referring to the concept of being burned or maybe what is also known as immolation. I cannot be certain, but I am thinking this is referring to the concept of Gehenna or the eternal punishment spoken of by Jesus in the New Testament.

Sepher Sipharah - This combination of words means scroll, book or letter.

Seraphim - Seraphim are mentioned in Isaiah as well are known to be the fiery serpents sent to bite the Hebrews will in the desert in the Exodus. They are considered class of angels who serve God, but in the use here it seems to make them more like a class of a living creature (zoon) of some kind vs. an actual angel.

Shachar - This word means 'to be black', and I think it is referring to the Zoroastrian god Aharman, who lives in the pit of the earth (i.e. Hell) in darkness. Aharman is not eternal in nature and is considered to be evil and is more or less like the Satan in Christianity.

Shekar- this means strong drink, and is clearly referring to a more potent form of alcohol. It is possible that it was some sort of early forms of distilled spirits or alcohol concentrate. What is interesting is that the Fallen Angels seem to imbue the substance with no harm to them, unlike us humans. Clearly the author or authors are trying to show that such strong drink can bring harm.

Shuchah - This word means pit, although in the context been used in this text, it would seem to be referring to some sort of spiritual prison for fallen angels. This would be consistent with parts of Revelations where certain demons, devils, and other horrid evil creatures are kept by God and the Angels for time in "the pit" only to be released later in accordance the plans for the end of time.

Takan - This word means to regulate, or measure, estimate or sometimes equalize or level.

Tame- this word means unclean. I think this is in reference to the idea that humans are sinful before the eyes of God.

Taqoa- this word means blast. This is a clear reference to the seven trumpet blasts mentioned in the Book of Revelations. Here they mention their destructive force and at the same time what appears to be the pronouncing of the coming of the Messiah. The Messianic prophecies begin at a time, which filled with much strife and death, so it would make sense that the proclamation of the coming of the Messiah would be associated with such things.

Tartan Uri Raphael - This is a direct reference to the Archangel Raphael mentioned in the book of Tobit, but the word 'tartan' means general or commander. Clearly this text is showing a rank difference between Uri who are commanders and Uri who are common soldiers (i.e. Guardian), with the exception of Elisheva the leader of the Uri. Interestingly, though you do not see this difference with Achim. The Achim evidently do not use specific rank titles; this could be because all of them equally answer to only one supreme commander-the Satan. Also the author could be showing the difference between a spirit world of order, and one of chaos.

Tehom - This word means "abyss" and is a clear reference to the same word mentioned in Genesis 1:2.

The Dabar - this means "the spoken". I think this is a reference to how creation was made in Genesis.

Togo Erets - Okay, this word is somewhat misspelled. Proper transliteration would be Tohu Erets, which basically means the "Chaos of Earth" and is a clear reference to again to Genesis 1:2.

Tsaatsuim Erets- this means sculptured earth, and an obvious reference to the created universe in Genesis. It is interesting how the writer(s) have made the distinction between the two forms of earth mentioned in Genesis; One of chaos and one of order.

Tsale - This word means "shades" and is clearly an older reference to the original concept of the inhabitants of the realm of the dead in early Jewish traditions.

Tsaphad- this is an interesting word because it means to draw together or contract but also can mean shriveled. I think in this sense it means a contractual process. Another words a marriage contract in the classic sense.

Tsir Uri Geber El - These words appear to be referring to the Angel Gabriel who in the bible is responsible for bringing messages from the Lord. In this particular case the word "tsir" means envoy and Gabriel's name is actually broken up into its original parts of Geber (man) and El (god) or Man of God.

Uri - The writer makes a clear distinction of the angels by using this word. The word means "God is my light" and hence the reference to the glowing armor. Clearly this is in reference to the distinction of the angels who follow God and those who are not following God, but the text seems to be following some other tradition in how the fallen angels are seen. It is a tradition I have not seen before, but it also could be the bias of the translation matrix.

Yago - This appears to be the friend of Zuriel. The word actually means "supplanter". He appears to be some lower class of worker angel.

Yahnah - This demon is not mentioned anywhere as far as I can tell, but the word means "the great oppressor". Clearly this demon is responsible for various forms of human enslavement, and hence I guess the name "great oppressor".

Yasha Erets Am- this translates into basically "Savoir of Earth's People"; and again another reference to the Messiah (i.e. Christ).

Yatsab - this means to present oneself or to take up one's seat at some meeting or place.

Yerushalem - This is the city of Jerusalem.

Zakah- this mean clean or pure, and again, I think this is in reference to the idea that some humans are not sinful before the eyes of God.

Same- this word means a device or plan.

Zanah- this word means harlot, but in this sense, I think it is referring more to sex itself. This would make sense since the author Zuriel is unfamiliar with the word, assuming that since he is supposed to be some sort of monk he has sworn off sex. Also, if Zuriel is also an angel as is suggested by earlier translations, then this also makes sense he wouldn't understand the word because to be honest angels (fallen or otherwise) typically are understood as not needing to have sex to reproduce since there is no need to reproduce at all. This was mentioned by Jesus in Matthew 22:30.

Zehman- this word already mentions in von Hemrick's notes as time. While this is a bit of a leap, I think this is the curse laid upon the man in Genesis (i.e. Adam) where he is to toil for food or another word we are to be bound by time. Interestingly, neither call nor shaman is understood by the writer, yet the words are used in the text.

Zoon- this word means "living creature" and again I have no idea what this is in reference to exactly especially with the word eternal before it. The only things I can come up with are the four living creatures mentioned in Revelations, but again a lot of this doesn't make sense. I do know that von Hemrick's notes seem be concerned about the construction of these eternal living creatures.

Zuriel - This appears to be the author of the text. While I think it is suggested that Zuriel is a fallen angel, I suspect the original author of the text is more than likely a collection of early Christian monastic scholars since the original text was discovered in the ruins of a monastery. This was not uncommon during early Christianity, and you see a lot of it occurring in Egypt with the Gnostic communities. Also Zuriel is the head of one of the Levitical clans known as Merari mentioned in Numbers 3:35 responsible for the transportation and care of the various components and parts of the tabernacle in part because they owned the wagons. So it is possible that the person who wrote this text may have been trying to link the knowledge of the text to responsibility concept mentioned but not necessarily to the person in Numbers 3:35.

Dates or Numbers

There are a series of what I believe are dates of any kind that are mentioned in the text, but the translation of these are just odd and really make no sense. But I will provide the Hebrew and word's meanings anyway in case someone with greater mathematically skill can come up with the dates they are referring to-

Dal (דַּל)- lean or needy.

Dalah (דָּלָה) -draw or lift up.

Dar (דָּר)- generation.

Dothan (דֹּתָן) - this is a place name in northern Samaria.

Darqon(דַּרְקוֹן) - this was the name of one of Solomon's servants.

Hege (הֵגֶי) - this was a eunuch of Xerxes.

Hayyah (הַיַּת) - calamity.

Zoth (זֹאת) - likewise.

Hemes (הֶמָסִים) - This word means dry twig or brushwood.

The Numbers Referring to People's Names

The one who talks of the poison infecting the "Church" (and I use this term very loosely) - 1478

The great prophet - 1560

The Revealer to the Americans - 180

The person whose number is 760 - This is a person who is a follower of Gur (who mentioned in an earlier translation), and who is evidently speaking on the 26th day of the Jewish Month of Iyyar sometime after Hayyah has occurred. Whoever this person is they will speak against God's regulated ways in a manner that is like that of Gur

Names Referring to a Person

Jar - (see above for the transliteration of meaning, but I suspect it referring to a person like how the dates do)

Brothers of Mastor - I am not certain who the Brothers are exactly, but they are evidently the Brothers of Egypt based on the translation since Mastor means Egypt.

Twin Sons of Apollo - I am not certain who this is in reference to exactly because the Greek God Apollo as far as I understand things was not known to have any sons. It is possible, and I am only speculating here, that Apollo may have been an actual person during the 4th Century when this community was around that had two sons that gave them trouble or something.

WHO IS OTTO VON HEMRICK?
DIE GEFALLENEN

He was the German archeologist who found the Die Gefallenen (the Book of Zuriel) in the ruins of a 4th Century Christian Monastery in the Syrian desert during the summer of 1932.

He was member of the Nazi group known as the Ahnenerbe, and through the help of Nazi code breakers and the use of an enigma machine was able to develop a translation matrix for the text's language he called

"Muttersprache" or the mother language.

Unfortunately, through a tragic experiment developed from the translations of the text he was reported to have died sometime in 1936.

Read more at www.angelmanuscripts.com

Seth Underwood

Can also be found

in the Joseph Street Digest

 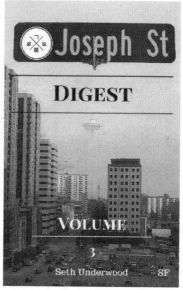

New Projects by Seth Underwood

71626320R00073

Made in the USA
San Bernardino, CA
18 March 2018